Photographic

A Wilson and Phillips-Lehman

Mystery

By

Ross Lowen

www.publishnation.co.uk

FRONT COVER ARTWORK
Front cover artwork by Joe Wilson
mail@jwilsonillustration.co.uk

DEDICATION

For Mark

ABOUT THE AUTHOR

Ross Lowen lives in Oxford and works part time at a modern
art gallery. Contact details: r.lowen@btopenworld.com

ACKNOWLEDGEMENTS

I would like to thank everyone who helped me write this book. My wife Fereshteh, Alexander and Julie for their encouragement and love, Christine for the information on nursing in the nineteen-seventies, Jonathan and Shaun for their friendship and providing a beautiful location in which to write part of the book, everyone at Publishnation, Joe Wilson for a superb cover design and Rob, for acting as a perfect sounding board whenever I came up with a new idea for the book.
Thanks to all of you.

CHAPTER ONE
OXFORD - SEPTEMBER 1973

It was early evening when Peter came around following the operation and he felt sick. It was the first time that he had been given an anesthetic and as he attempted to lift himself up to be sick, a nurse rushed across to his bed and gently eased him back on to his pillows.

"You must lay flat Peter, if you feel as though you want to be sick you can roll onto your side." the nurse said.

The nurse's voice was soft with a foreign accent, but Peter couldn't detect which country she was from. He lay back and listened to the truncated music, which drifted through the open windows of the ward. Of course, he remembered, it was St Giles Fair! He had covered it for the Oxford Mail last year during his probation period as a trainee reporter. First held in 1624 and always falling on the Monday and Tuesday, following the first Sunday after St Giles day, the first day of September. Sidney Newman, the editor of the Mail, had been impressed with the research he had undertaken.

"Please tell me if you feel sick again Peter, I will be sitting with you until you fall asleep. It is very important that you do not sit up until your eye has healed." said the foreign accent.

Peter's left eye was covered with a patch to protect it following surgery and unless he turned to one side, which made him feel nauseous, he could barely see the nurse with the foreign accent. The truncated music from St Giles Fair continued, with Freda Payne repeatedly singing Band of Gold, only interrupted by the excited screams of the children on the fairground rides.

The following morning, Mr. Hawtrey entered Doyle Ward, with his usual assorted entourage, to do his rounds. On this occasion, it included Chief Nursing Officer Arbuthnot, who fitted the stereotypical image of a Matron perfectly, being a plump, stern looking woman, Ward Sister Jenny Roberts, an attractive, slim blonde woman in her early forties and three junior doctors, all male. Mr. Hawtrey, as usual, was immaculately dressed, *Gieves and Hawkes* navy blue suit with a discrete pinstripe, starched white Jermyn Street shirt, Oxford brogues and an extremely colourful flower patterned tie, just to demonstrate that the Sixties hadn't completely passed him by. He had become Senior Consultant three years ago and was enjoying the prestige which came with the position. An easy charm with the patients, serious and courteous with Matron and the other hospital staff and when the mood took him, flirtatious with the younger female staff, Bernard Hawtrey oozed confidence. He was also a brilliant eye surgeon.

His entourage assembled behind him at the foot of Peter Wilson's bed and whilst the consultant read through Peter's notes, Matron and Sister Roberts discussed their morning's duties. The junior doctors shuffled around to the right hand side of the bed, where Nurse Taraneh Saderzadeh was standing, slightly nervously, it was the first time she had come across Mr. Hawtrey.

"So, young Peter, recovering well after the operation? Good, good!" Mr. Hawtrey said without looking up from his notes.

Peter was about to answer but, like most of his questions when meeting patients, Bernard Hawtrey didn't expect an answer, it was purely a rhetorical question.

"You had a nasty accident young man," he continued, looking at Peter over the top of his glasses, "hit the old bonce on the windscreen, not wearing a seatbelt I expect, in future, *clunk click, every trip* my boy!" Hawtrey smiled and noticed, with pleasure, that the young doctors were enjoying his performance this morning.

"We brought you here to the Eye Hospital because you had what's commonly known as a detached retina Peter. The retina is the light sensitive tissue lining the back of the eye and yours had separated from the layer beneath, the impact of your head hitting the windscreen caused the detachment I would think." Hawtrey was well into his stride by now and enjoying himself, "we operated yesterday and I stitched it up for you! Dissolvable stitches, so we don't have to take the little blighters out later on."

"Will I be able to see properly again?" Peter interrupted, it was the first time he'd spoken and unusually for him, he felt slightly nervous.

Mr. Hawtrey noticed that the foreign looking young nurse, stood to Peter's side, looked sad after hearing his question.

"Your right eye is fine Peter and has good sight and to a large extent will compensate for any loss of sight you experience in your left eye. However, it's too early, at this stage, to say how successful the operation was and how much sight in your left eye we've saved. I have high hopes for it! But, we'll know more over the coming days." Mr. Hawtrey's tone was kinder and slightly subdued.

"Right Matron," he continued, "Peter requires some special care for the next two weeks whilst he recovers from the surgery and his other minor injuries and for at least the first week, he must not get out of bed or, sit up. Food by mouth, but spoon fed I'm afraid."

"Yes Mr. Hawtrey," replied Matron, "Sister Roberts, could you please brief us on the arrangements you've put in place so far."

"Certainly Matron," Sister Roberts said and Hawtrey smiled and looked over at her approvingly as she went through the arrangements, "I have assigned trainee Nurse Saderzadeh to provide special care for Mr. Wilson during his stay with us. Sister Hall is on night shift for two weeks and has been appraised of the situation."

All eyes turned towards the young nurse, who, although nervous, looked dignified and nodded confirming that she understood her duties.

"Saderzadeh, it sounds like a Middle Eastern name." remarked Mr. Hawtrey, pleased with himself.

"Yes sir, I am Persian." the nurse replied.

"Nurse Saderzadeh has been training with us for nearly three months and is making good progress," Sister Roberts continued, "I'm confident she will take good care of Mr. Wilson."

"Yes, I'm sure you have everything in hand Sister." Hawtrey smiled and once again, caught Jenny Robert's eye.

"Shall we move on Mr. Hawtrey, you have a very busy morning." reminded Matron.

"Yes thank you Margery, quite right, busy morning." agreed Hawtrey and with that, they were gone, Matron Margery Arbuthnot secretly pleased with herself to be on first name terms with such an eminent consultant.

Peter lay flat on his bed wondering how on earth he would occupy himself for the next two weeks or, possibly even longer. His mind drifted and he thought back to his upbringing in Birmingham. An only child, he was born five years after the end of the Second World War. His parents were what he would describe as educated working class. His father had spent his life working on the railways and now, aged 65, was approaching retirement. A quiet shy man, Stanley Wilson, never Stan, had taken pride in providing for his small family. He was a member of the Birmingham Historical Society and their small terraced house in Selly Oak, a suburb of Birmingham, was crammed full of local history books concerning the city. Stanley's other love was music. He played the acoustic guitar well and he had a large collection of jazz records which he would listen to at the weekends, when he wasn't working. Stanley had met his wife, Dorothy, shortly after the end of the war, she had travelled to Birmingham from Glasgow, her birthplace, in 1943 to be near her sister who was living in Selly Oak. She met Stanley in 1946, whilst she was working as a waitress in one of the Municipal restaurants, which had sprung up throughout the country during the war years to provide people with good, reasonably priced, nutritious food. They were married within twelve months and Peter was born on May Day 1950.

Peter's childhood was a happy one, he was popular at school and loved by his parents at home. Stanley and Dorothy noticed that Peter had started to read and write from an early age and Stanley encouraged him by taking him to the local library on Saturday mornings. Peter would choose a book and invariably, would have finished it by the following Saturday. Whilst Stanley was proud that he had always provided for his family through his job on the railways, he dearly wanted something better for Peter and he knew that education was the key. Peter passed the eleven-plus and went to the local Grammar School, where he excelled in English literature, history and sport before applying and succeeding in gaining a scholarship to study at Oxford University. Throughout his childhood, Peter had also taken an interest in his father's collection of jazz records, particularly the LPs, which were a much better sound quality than the older 78s. He had become a teenager in 1963, which coincided with the popularity of The Beatles and The Rolling Stones, amongst others, and he persuaded Stanley to teach him to play guitar. By the time he was fifteen he was playing in a pop group, formed at his Grammar school, and much to his father's dismay he started to grow his hair long!

Peter enjoyed Oxford, social mobility was prevalent during the 1960s and although, at times, he was teased over his strong Brummie accent, there was tangible evidence of changing attitudes. It helped that he was good at sport. He played football to a good standard and more importantly, he rowed for his college, which gained him acceptance amongst the students from more privileged backgrounds. Peter read politics at Oxford, but he had made up his mind during his first year that he wanted to become a journalist. He graduated in 1971 with a first class honours degree and Stanley and Dorothy attended his graduation ceremony, agreeing it was one of the happiest days of their lives.

One aspect of Peter's time whilst up at Oxford which was not so successful was his relationship with girls. He rarely lacked any attention from girls, after all, he was tall, quite good looking and sporty. However, he did lack confidence when with them. He tended to hide this lack of confidence by drinking too much and for a while, he gained a reputation at college for being a bit of a boozer. Thankfully, he was what is often described as a 'happy drunk' and his drinking did not result in any aggressive behavior. The problem Peter encountered, was that the girls he mixed with at college tended to be from nice middle class backgrounds and whilst he did feel attracted towards one or two of them and struck up relationships with them, sex was not particularly enjoyable and left him, for some reason, feeling guilty. Years later, when he thought about his time at Oxford, he would come to understand that he had experienced difficulty distinguishing between love and sex. However, for the time being, Peter overcame these problems by drinking a bit too much and by meeting girls from the other 'side' of town. Oxford had always been split between 'Town and Gown', as it was known and the pubs were generally divided along these lines. Peter met girls from a similar background to his own in the Town pubs and when he was honest with himself, he felt more comfortable in their company. He found that he drank less and sex was more enjoyable for him and hopefully, for whoever his partner was at the time! On leaving university, Peter was offered a position working as a junior reporter for the local newspaper, the Oxford Mail. He had envisaged moving straight to London to try his luck on getting a position with one of the national papers in Fleet Street, but felt that the experience he would gain working as a reporter on a local paper would stand him in good stead for the future. He covered local events for the paper, such as St Giles Fair, less serious court cases and local amateur football matches and it was driving to report on one of these matches, that he was involved in the car accident that resulted in his stay at the Radcliffe Infirmary.

CHAPTER TWO

TWO TIMING

Nurse Taraneh Saderzadeh wheeled the trolley containing Peter's lunch and stopped next to his bed. He'd had nothing to eat since the cup of tea, drank through a straw, and a slice of toast for breakfast and he felt very hungry.

"I have brought you your lunch Peter, cottage pie followed by apple pie and custard." Nurse Saderzadeh announced.

Peter turned slightly on the bed so he could get a better look at the Persian nurse, whilst she started to arrange his lunch on the over-bed table. Although his left eye was completely covered by an eye patch and the vision in his right eye was a little blurred, Peter thought the nurse looked about the same age as him, she was slim, quite short with an olive complexion. He noticed she had dark brown eyes and jet black shoulder length hair, if he hadn't known better he thought she could easily have been from the Mediterranean region, perhaps Greek or, even Italian.

"Thank you nurse, I'm starving." Peter smiled.

"I am going to spoon feed you with the cottage pie and runner beans first Peter, here is another pillow so you can lift your head a little, but you must not sit up, you heard what Mr. Hawtrey said. If you feel yourself choking just tap my arm," the nurse told him.

Peter noticed that, whilst she had quite a strong accent, her English was excellent and spoken softly.

"Where did you learn your English nurse?" Peter asked, it's very good."

Taraneh started to feed Peter and told him that, before coming to Oxford to start her training three months ago, she had lived in London for five years. Her father worked at the Iranian Embassy in Kensington and she lived with him nearby. She had come to London when she was fifteen and had attended a private girls' school in St John's Wood until she was eighteen. She had always dreamt of becoming a nurse in England since she was a child in Tehran, although her family had told her they were unsure whether it was a suitable profession for her. However, she told Peter, she has a strong character, like a lot of Persian women, and had managed to persuade her father to let her come to England!

The cottage pie was soon gone and Peter was enjoying the apple pie and custard when Sister Roberts appeared at his bedside.

"Your mother has been on the telephone Peter and she said she is coming to visit you this evening with your father." Sister Roberts told him. Peter looked surprised.

"How on earth did they know I'm here?" he spluttered, custard dripping from his chin.

"Apparently, when the police and ambulance crew pulled you out of the car they discovered you worked for the Oxford Mail, who gave the police details of your next of kin." Sister Roberts replied frowning.

"You should have told them yourself Peter!" Nurse Saderzadeh told him crossly when Sister Roberts had gone.

"Yes, I know, but I didn't want to worry them." Peter replied sadly.

Stanley and Dorothy Wilson got off the train at Oxford Station at six o'clock, evening visiting times at the Radcliffe Infirmary were between seven and eight and they would have time to see Peter and catch their return train home to Birmingham afterwards. They walked from the station to the hospital, following the directions Sister Roberts had kindly given them over the telephone. The last

9

time they had visited Oxford had been for Peter's graduation ceremony, a much happier occasion. This felt more daunting and although they had spoken of little else since they had received the visit from the police, they were quiet as they made their way on foot through Oxford.

On arrival at the Radcliffe, they were allowed in to see Peter immediately and on seeing him lying flat on his back with a large patch covering his left eye and bruising on his forehead, Dorothy burst into tears, leant over the bed and hugged him.

"You should have got a message to us earlier son," Stanley said quietly, "it was a terrible shock for your mother when the police turned up on the doorstep."

"Sorry dad." Peter mumbled and he was really sorry, he felt awful.

Dorothy unpacked her bag, she'd brought grapes, oranges, a bottle of Lucozade and a home-made lemon meringue pie, Peter's favourite.

"Thanks mum, that's really kind of you, I'll call the nurse and she can put the fruit in a bowl." Peter said cheering up a bit. He told them what he remembered about the accident, waking up in Casualty and then being transferred to the Eye Hospital for his operation yesterday evening.

"There's nothing to worry about mum, they've told me that I'll make a full recovery and be up and about in no time." Peter lied and as he was telling them about the visit from Mr. Hawtrey earlier in the day, Nurse Saderzadeh arrived carrying a large fruit bowl, she had seen Mrs. Wilson unpacking her bag.

"This is Nurse Saderzadeh, she's looking after me during my stay here," Peter informed his parents smiling, "she is originally from Persia!"

"I am pleased to meet you Mr. and Mrs. Wilson." Taraneh said.

10

"We're pleased to meet you as well dear," Dorothy replied, "please help yourself to some fruit, I've made Peter a lemon meringue pie, do you think you could put it in the fridge for me?"

"Of course Mrs. Wilson, I'll do it right away," Taraneh replied. "Would you like me to bring you both a cup of tea?"

"No thank you dear, we had tea at the station." Dorothy said.

Just as Taraneh was about to leave with the lemon meringue pie, Stanley stood up, smiled at her and in a broad Brummie accent spoke to Taraneh in Farsi telling her he was pleased to meet her.

"Az molaghat-e shoma khosh bagtam!"

Peter looked surprised, Dorothy smiled and Taraneh looked delighted.

"Kheily mamnoon, khoshbaktam, chetori Mr. Wilson?" Taraneh asked Stanley how he was.

"Khobam merci." Stanley replied, telling her he is fine.

"What an earth is going on?" Peter asked, looking surprised.

"Your father was stationed in Persia during the war Peter and he learnt some Farsi, hasn't he ever told you?" Dorothy smiled.

"No he hasn't!" Peter replied looking slightly disgruntled.

Taraneh was still laughing, when Stanley explained that he had spent nearly two years in Abadan, protecting the oil fields, during the war when he picked up some rudimentary Farsi.

"What else haven't you told me about yourself dad?" Peter asked, now smiling.

"I will leave you with your lovely parents Peter, please use the bell if you need anything, goodbye Mrs. Wilson and hodahafez Mr. Wilson."

When Taraneh had left, Stanley told Peter that he was in good hands with Nurse Saderzadeh.

11

"Yes, I think you are Peter!" Dorothy laughed.

Peter had been pleased to see his parents and seeing them brought home to him how fortunate he had been to avoid more serious injuries during the accident. Nurse Saderzadeh had visited him before she finished her shift and told him how lucky he was to have such caring, loving parents and she could tell that they were clearly good people. She was right, they are 'good people' thought Peter and it made him reflect on some of his own failings and wonder whether he would one day be described as a 'good person'.

With this in mind, he remembered the only other occasion that he had visited the Radcliffe Infirmary, which had been under embarrassing circumstances, during his last year at university. He had been dating a fellow student, a pretty girl called Emily. She came from a very different background to Peter, having grown up in a large house in Surrey, her father a stockbroker and her mother a local magistrate. Emily had been going through a rebellious period which many students, particularly from her background, experienced. She was drinking too much, usually champagne or, sparkling wine when her monthly allowance from her parents had nearly all gone. She smoked the occasional joint and Peter had suspicions that cannabis wasn't the only drug she was taking, although he had no evidence. When he asked her about it she would become angry, so he didn't pursue the matter with her. Peter had smoked cannabis a few times, but didn't really enjoy the experience. Unusually for the time, he didn't smoke cigarettes and he thought that this was probably the main reason he didn't enjoy cannabis. Later on in life, Peter would remember how different the attitude towards drugs was during the sixties and seventies. Many at the time thought that they were liberating and there was a feeling amongst those who took drugs, that it was 'cool'. This view was reinforced by the music and fashion scene throughout this period. Although they rarely socialised together, Emily's friends were very different to the crowd Peter mixed with, they had been sleeping together for about two months. However, whilst the sex was enjoyable, Peter's feelings of guilt would always emerge soon afterwards and as a result of this, he had started dating another girl from East Oxford, a 'Town girl'. He had met Shirley during a night out drinking with the lads from a local football team, for whom he turned out on some Sunday mornings. Shirley was a hairdresser at a salon in Cowley, a suburb of Oxford and Peter would telephone her every Wednesday morning, whilst she was at work, to see whether she would be free that evening. Shirley's mother went to bingo on most Wednesday evenings and they would have the house to themselves for a few hours. Peter had asked Shirley about her father, but all she told him was that he worked away, so Peter didn't ask her again! Invariably, they would meet at a pub on the Cowley Road near to where Shirley lived at opening time, which was seven o'clock. Peter would have a couple of pints of bitter and Shirley would usually drink Gold Label, otherwise known as barley wine, which was strong and her favourite tipple. They would wait until eight o'clock, when bingo started at the local Community Centre, and then retire to Shirley's house for a very enjoyable evening! Shirley was five years older than Peter and very good looking. She had done a bit of modelling for *Kays*, the mail order catalogue, over the past few years and Peter encouraged her to pursue this as a full time career, but like a lot of young people from her background she seemed to lack confidence in herself. Peter liked Shirley a lot, she was bright, funny and engaging and if he was asked to describe her in one word, he would say she was 'earthy!' Interestingly, in contrast to his relationship with Emily, he felt no guilt following sex with Shirley and their arrangement continued for a couple of months. Peter knew it was wrong two timing Shirley and Emily and he was sure that his parents would have been disappointed with him, although he was equally sure that Shirley probably wouldn't have cared less!

Coincidently, it was on Wednesday morning, just before he was about to telephone Shirley at the hairdresser's, that Peter felt an unpleasant burning sensation when he urinated. As it turned out, when he eventually called Shirley, she told him that there wasn't much point in him coming to see her that evening because she had her 'period'. Peter offered to come anyway and suggested that they could just have a drink together, but Shirley just laughed and said let's just wait until next week! Peter smiled to himself when he put down the phone, he was very fond of Shirley and really would have enjoyed it if they had just met for a drink. More worryingly, over the next few days Peter's symptoms got worse, the burning sensation was more painful each time he went to the toilet and he had noticed some discharge when he woke up during the night. He made an appointment to see his doctor, telling the receptionist that it was urgent, and was immediately referred to the, walk in, Venereal Diseases Clinic at the Radcliffe Infirmary. Peter was horrified and felt ashamed, he also felt scared, but he realised that there was nothing else for it but to go there straight away.

The VD Clinic, as it was commonly known, was easily found from the Woodstock Road and following registration, Peter found himself sitting in the waiting room with six or seven other patients. The first surprise was that there were men and women waiting to be seen. Whilst he hadn't given it much thought before he arrived at the clinic, for some unknown reason he had assumed that all the patients would be men and young, like himself. That was the second surprise, everyone else in the waiting room were much older than him. The men looked as though they were all in their forties or fifties and the two women present must have been well in to their thirties. In fact, due to his naivety, for a moment Peter thought that he must be in the wrong waiting room and discretely asked the man sat next to him if he was in the right clinic! The man, who was quite sharply dressed, considered Peter for a moment, smiled and then in a louder than expected voice said, "Yep, this is for the Clap son!"

Peter detected a few smiles breaking out around him.

He was seen by a nurse who examined him and took a sample, using a swab, before sending him back to the waiting room. After a wait that seemed like an eternity, Peter was called in to see a doctor who, unceremoniously, told him that he had contracted gonorrhoea! The remainder of the consultation passed by in a bit of a blur, but Peter remembered being given a large dose of anti-biotics and being told that the symptoms should start to clear up within two or three days. His sense of relief at this news was tempered, when the doctor gave him a handful of leaflets and told him he must pass them on to anyone he'd had sexual intercourse with over the past few weeks. Peter left the clinic feeling thoroughly miserable. His first thought, which he later felt ashamed of, was that he must have contracted the infection from Shirley. It never even entered his mind that he could have caught it from Emily.

Peter would never find out who passed the infection on to him. He did as the doctor had told him and arranged to see Shirley the next day during her lunch break from the hairdresser's. They met in the greasy spoon café across the road from the salon. Peter told Shirley that he had contracted VD, he couldn't bring himself to say gonorrhoea. Looking back, Peter thought Shirley's response was typical of her.

"Oh, you poor darling!" she said reaching out to hold his hand.

"The doctor asked me to give you this leaflet Shirley," Peter said sadly, "I think you should think about getting yourself tested."

"Well, I'll read it tonight and see what I need to do." Shirley replied and then said something he would always remember, "This doesn't mean we're going to break up does it Pete?"

The meeting with Emily was in total contrast. Peter visited her in the flat she shared with another female student just off the Banbury Road.

"How dare you! I don't want your filthy leaflet......Get out!" she screamed at him.

Peter made one more last effort suggesting that she should really get herself tested, but it was to no avail. She had slammed the front door behind him and before he knew it, he was walking back up the Banbury Road towards his college.

CHAPTER THREE

TARANEH SADERZADEH

Taraneh Saderzadeh woke in the Nurses' Home at six o'clock each morning. Her room on the first floor was small, but included a fridge and tea making facilities. A communal kitchen for all the nurses to use was on the ground floor. She made herself weak tea in a samovar, which she had brought with her when she came to England from Iran, and drank it with one sugar cube. She had found a delicatessen, one of the first in Oxford, that sold Greek feta cheese and she ate this for her breakfast with cherry jam, which she made herself. When she was working, her main meal of the day would be taken at the hospital. She missed Persian food, but enjoyed some of the traditional English dishes they served in the canteen such as shepherd's pie, Lancashire hot pot and chicken casserole.

Taraneh was born in Iran in 1953 and had grown up in Tehran, the youngest of three daughters to relatively wealthy parents. Her father, Mohsen Saderzadeh, had been educated in England shortly after the Second World War and had prospered when he returned to Iran during the nineteen-fifties and sixties as the Shah introduced a modernisation program for the country. He was a career diplomat, specialising in defence matters, and by the time he was posted to the embassy in London, he had already served terms in the Iranian embassies in Spain and France. As well as his native language, Farsi, he was fluent in English, French and Spanish. His wife, Farah, the daughter of a wealthy bazaari, or merchant, from Tehran was content to look after her three daughters whilst her husband was

17

posted abroad, making the occasional visit to Europe to see him when the mood took her.

From an early age, Taraneh had known she was different to her elder sisters, she had a particularly strong character and when she made her mind up to do something, nothing would stop her. This occasionally brought her into conflict with her older sisters, who described her as stubborn. However, the whole family knew, she was her father's favourite. She had dreamt of becoming a nurse since reading a book as a young child about nurses working in a London hospital and when her father told the family about his posting to London, she instinctively knew that this was her chance and even though she was barely fifteen years old, she was going to take it! Her mother and sisters tried to persuade her that nursing was not the best profession for her and that she should have loftier ambitions. Taraneh would not listen to them and begged her father to take her with him to London. She had her plan already worked out, she would go to school in London whilst her father was working at the embassy and when she was old enough, apply to become a student nurse. She had read that at this time in England, training to become a nurse was 'on the job', rather than at college, and this would suit her down to the ground. At first, her father laughed and didn't take her seriously, but she pestered him for weeks before he left for London, even providing him with a written plan of how she intended to achieve her ambition, and in the end he relented, as she knew he would!

London in 1968 was an exciting place to be for a teenager, even one as young as Taraneh, who was just fifteen. Her father had found a place for her at a private girls' school in St John's Wood. Taraneh was delighted that her plan was working out. She already spoke rudimentary English, but knew that she would have to improve dramatically before she would be accepted as a student nurse. Taraneh excelled at school and was extremely

18

popular with the other girls and at seventeen she became head girl! She left at eighteen with three A Level passes and started applying for positions to become a student nurse. At first she was met with a number of rejections which at first annoyed her, but ultimately made her even more determined to achieve her ambition. When school finished, Taraneh took a job working at a nursery in Kensington near to the apartment she shared with her father and following this, took up a live-in job as a nanny for a wealthy young couple and their new born baby in Hampstead. It was whilst nannying that she was finally accepted to take up a position as a student nurse in Oxford at the Radcliffe Infirmary. It was 1973.

Taraneh finished her breakfast, put on her nurse's uniform, including the paper hat and starched white apron and knocked on the door of the apartment across the corridor to see whether Rita, another student nurse, was ready to take the short walk to the Radcliffe. Rita was the complete opposite of Taraneh, untidy and disorganised, with a compulsive nature. They had started as student nurses at the Radcliffe on the same day and had become good friends. Rita, a Liverpudlian, was forever telling Taraneh how beautiful she was with her dark complexion and big brown eyes and Taraneh loved to listen to Rita speaking with her strong scouse accent.

"Just coming Tara love!" shouted Rita, she was always rushing first thing in the morning Taraneh thought. A few minutes later they were walking down the Woodstock Road together towards the hospital.

"So Tara, I've heard on the grapevine that he's quite dishy!" Rita said smiling.

"Who and what is dishy?" asked Taraneh.

"The young reporter you've been looking after," Rita continued, "he's very good looking so I've heard!"

"Well, he is quite handsome I suppose, or will be when the bruising on his head has gone." Taraneh could feel herself blushing and Rita picked up on it immediately.

"I thought so, you've got a crush on him haven't you!" teased Rita. "You can't hide it from me Tara love, I can tell, under all that demure behaviour you fancy him, you're a dark horse you are!"

"Rita, I have absolutely no idea what you are talking about," Taraneh told her, sounding as if she was still head girl, "crush, dishy, dark horses, what is all this nonsense?"

Rita smiled and Taraneh continued trying her upmost not to laugh, "You know perfectly well Rita it is against the hospital regulations for us to have any sort of relationship with doctors or patients."

"Well if that young doctor in ENT asks me out I won't be saying no!" Rita said.

"You are terrible Rita!" Taraneh laughed.

If the truth were known, Taraneh had become fond of Peter and it worried her slightly. She was supposed to be training to be a nurse and she suddenly finds she has feelings for the first young man she has had to look after!

Peter's stay in hospital would last three weeks. The first week was the most difficult, because he wasn't allowed to sit up. However, he was surprised at how quickly he fell into a routine, even under difficult circumstances. He found that the time actually passed quite quickly, he would be woken very early in the morning most days at about six thirty by the sound of the cleaners. Breakfast was served at seven thirty and later in the morning the doctors and sometimes the consultants would do their rounds of the wards. Peter looked forward to watching Mr. Hawtrey in action, it was a performance, with a full supporting cast and Bernard Hawtrey was the star! Lunch was at midday and some patients took a nap between one and two o'clock. Visiting times were between three and four o'clock and again between seven and eight. Peter's parents visited whenever they could and were pleased to see their son was making a good recovery. According to Mr. Hawtrey, the speed with which they had operated on Peter had probably saved about half of the sight in his left eye.

It was at meal times that Peter got to know Nurse Taraneh better, particularly during his first week in hospital when she spoon fed him. Midway through that first week, they removed his eye patch and he noticed that the swelling and bruising around the other eye and his forehead had begun to reduce. For the first time since the accident he found that he could focus a lot better. Previously, whilst he could recognise people, their features had been blurred. Now that he could see more clearly, he realised how attractive the nurse was who had been looking after him. During meal times, nurse Taraneh would do most of the talking whilst he ate and Peter was interested to hear about her life in Iran, before she came to live in England. He was particularly impressed that she had left behind what sounded like a very privileged upbringing, with servants looking after her family, for a relatively simple life abroad training to be a nurse. It was during one of these conversations, the day that Mr. Hawtrey had told Peter that he would shortly be able to sit up in bed and feed himself, that Taraneh told him an unusual story, that in forty years' time would have a dramatic effect on his life and on those around him.

CHAPTER FOUR

THE NANNY

It was on a cold, wet afternoon in January 1973 that Taraneh Saderzadeh arrived, with a small suitcase, at the large house in Hampstead to take up her duties as a nanny. She was disappointed that, at this stage, she been unsuccessful in fulfilling her dream of becoming a nurse and she saw her appointment as a nanny, very much as a temporary position. She had no idea that her application for the position of student nurse at the Radcliffe Infirmary, which she had posted the previous weekend, would be successful and in six months' time she would be starting her new life in Oxford.

The job as a nanny had come right out of the blue and was mainly due to her father's connections through his job. Mohsen Saderzadeh worked long hours at the embassy in Kensington and on three or four evenings each week he would be out for dinner either entertaining or, being entertained. Taraneh had become used to the demanding nature of her father's job as a diplomat and whilst she was uncertain of what he actually did, she acknowledged that he was playing an important role on behalf of their country. It was extremely rare for her father to bring work home to their luxurious apartment in Kensington, but over the Christmas holiday of 1972 he had invited some guests to a cocktail party. The guests included a number of English Members of Parliament and following the party, to Taraneh's surprise, her father asked her if she would be interested in working as a nanny for one of the young MPs and his wife, who were about to have their first child.

22

Taraneh's job at the nursery was about to come to an end and she thought that a change of scenery would be welcome, whilst she waited to see whether her applications at a number of hospitals to become a student nurse would be successful. She was also pleased to be able to help her father, who obviously had some kind of connection, through his job with the young MP.

Taraneh was invited in by the housekeeper Mrs. Jeffreys, a pleasant woman in her early fifties.

"You must be Taraneh, what a beautiful name!" she smiled, "come through and I'll show you up to your room, baby Simon is asleep and Margaret is having a nap as well."

It was a large Victorian detached house with a beautiful mature west facing garden to the rear. Taraneh's room overlooked the garden and was next door to the nursery, where baby Simon was asleep.

"Robert is down in Sussex visiting his constituency today," Mrs. Jeffreys continued, "why don't you unpack and then come down to the kitchen, I'm baking some fruit scones and they're almost ready."

Although the house was in London, the kitchen could have been in a large farmhouse in the countryside. A large oak table and chairs dominated the kitchen and Taraneh sat with Mrs. Jeffreys drinking tea and enjoying the fruit scones, which were served with raspberry jam. After twenty minutes or so Margaret appeared and introduced herself to Taraneh. She was a tall, elegant woman with long dark hair in her early thirties, but she looked very tired and Taraneh noticed that, at times, she looked a little anxious. However, Taraneh put this down to the fact that only five days had passed since she had given birth! Mrs. Jeffreys busied herself in the kitchen and Taraneh followed Margaret back up to the nursery, where baby Simon was still sleeping.

"He's beautiful." Taraneh whispered and Margaret nodded.

"Let him sleep for a bit longer, he was up most of the night, I think he's struggling to get used to the bottled milk. Come down to the study and I'll run through your duties with you." Margaret said.

And so, Taraneh's short career as a nanny was underway. Margaret, a scientist based at one of the Universities in London, was keen to get back to work and did so just over a week after Taraneh arriving. Taraneh thought it slightly strange that a mother with a newborn child would want to return to work so quickly, but presumed that this was normal in England. Margaret would leave for work each morning after helping Taraneh feed baby Simon and return between six and seven o'clock each evening, when she would help put him to bed. Taraneh was tasked with feeding baby Simon during the night, except at weekends when Margaret would take charge. Whenever the opportunity arose, Taraneh would take a nap during the day. She would have lunch and dinner in the kitchen with Mrs. Jeffreys, who lived in a small annex to the side of the house. She was an excellent cook and the two of them struck up a good relationship and at times, Taraneh felt as though she had a second mother!

Taraneh saw very little of Robert, during the week he spent most of his time either in his office at the Ministry of Defence or, in the Houses of Parliament in Westminster. At the weekends, more often than not, he would drive down to Sussex and stay at the family's country cottage in his constituency. On those weekends that he did stay in London, he and Margaret often entertained at home and it was on one of those occasions, that Taraneh inadvertently overheard a terrible argument between the young couple that several months later she would recount to Peter, during his stay in hospital.

A dinner party for some close friends had been arranged for the Saturday evening and Taraneh who had been nannying for nearly two months by this time, helped Mrs

Jeffreys in the kitchen prepare for the event. Taraneh had noticed that Margaret had been on edge during the day and was clearly not looking forward to the party. Margaret's behaviour when she was with baby Simon had surprised her a little. Both parents were always kind and caring when they were with him, but Taraneh had had noticed that there seemed to be a lack of emotional attachment between the parents and the baby. It was more noticeable with Margaret, but that was probably because Robert spent so little time at home, she thought. Taraneh rarely dwelt upon these feelings and put them down to her own lack of understanding of how different cultures dealt with small children, but it had left a nagging doubt in her mind. Those doubts were to resurface in the early hours of Sunday morning.

Taraneh had heard the guests leave at about midnight when she checked on baby Simon and then returned next door to her own room and drifted off to sleep. She awoke suddenly about an hour later, the baby was crying. She was out of bed in seconds, slipped into the nursery and picked up baby Simon, comforting him. He was calm again in seconds and Taraneh wondered whether he'd had a bad dream. It was only then that she heard raised voices downstairs and for a moment, strangely, felt pleased with herself that it was the baby's cries that had woken her, rather than the parents arguing. They couldn't have heard the baby crying because the shouting continued. Taraneh fed the baby from a bottle she had prepared earlier and settled him back in his cot. As she returned to her room she stopped on the landing and heard Robert lecturing Margaret in a loud voice.

"I haven't spent the past ten years climbing the greasy pole to have my career snatched away from me because of your stupidity! Do you have any idea how dull Defence meetings can be? Day after bloody day, boring repetitive meetings lasting long into the night with dreadful civil servants and then at weekends, it's down to the constituency to open some bloody fete organised by a bunch of mad old biddies from the Women's Institute! And then there's the surgery, an endless stream of miserable middle class, middle aged men complaining about some proposed by-pass, asking me how I'm going to get it stopped!" Robert continued shouting, "well, I'm telling you Margaret that you need to forget all about this stupid idea. Do you really think, in your wildest dreams, that you can walk into Hampstead nick and say hello officer, I think I've made a terrible mistake and have the wrong baby! Oh, and by the way, my husband's a Member of Parliament who's being tipped by the London Evening Standard as a future Prime Minister!"

Taraneh could hear sobbing coming from the kitchen downstairs and in a slightly quieter, but threatening tone Robert ended his diatribe, "I'm telling you, if you think you can pass this off as carelessness, you've got another think coming. You can't put the toothpaste back in the tube Margaret, what's done, is done and remember we made a pact never to mention this."

Taraneh tiptoed back to her room and returned to bed feeling confused and unsettled, all the time thinking, what did he mean, 'have the wrong baby'?

CHAPTER FIVE

THE YOUNG REPORTERS

Peter was finally discharged from the Radcliffe Infirmary after spending three weeks in the hospital. Bernard Hawtrey had paid him a last visit on the morning of his discharge. He told Peter that he was delighted by the speed of his recovery and whilst he would be left with what the surgeon described as peripheral vision in his left eye, his right eye was perfect and would, to a large degree, compensate for the reduced vision in his left eye. However, Mr. Hawtrey recommended that, in future, Peter refrain from contact sports such as rugby, football and boxing and remembers to wear a seatbelt whilst driving.

"I'm sure there are plenty of other activities a healthy, good looking young man like you can indulge in!" Hawtrey suggested with a smile. Peter noticed Sister Jenny Roberts blush and then, with a flourish, he had moved on to the next patient along with his entourage.

Stanley and Dorothy Wilson arrived at the Radcliffe just after lunch. Peter had decided to spend a week at home with his parents in Birmingham, before returning to his job at the Oxford Mail. He had spoken to the editor of the paper earlier that day and was pleased to be told that they were looking forward to seeing him back at work.

Before his parents arrived, Nurse Taraneh came to see him. She had been assigned different duties since Peter had been able to sit up in bed and feed himself. She told him that she could only stay for five minutes but wanted to wish him luck before he was discharged.

"Please pass on my best wishes to your lovely parents as well Peter." she said.

"Thank you Nurse Saderzadeh, I will, I can tell you that you're very popular with them! I will miss you and I don't know what I'd have done without you these past few weeks!" Peter smiled making a joke of it, but deep down, he really meant it. He felt that they had become quite close, particularly since she had told him the story of the unusual events in Hampstead when she was a nanny.

"I'll be back in Oxford within a week or so and perhaps we could meet for a coffee and a chat one day?" he asked.

"I would like that very much Peter." she smiled and then she was gone.

Peter was thoroughly spoilt at home in Birmingham. Dorothy cooked him all of his favourite dishes, cottage pie, Lancashire hot pot, Scotch broth and of course, lemon meringue pie. He noticed, not for the first time, that his parents were ageing, his father would be retiring later in the year after a lifetime working on the railways. A quiet intelligent man, Stanley commented that retirement would give him more time to read, tend to his allotment and help Dorothy around the house. Nurse Saderzadeh was right Peter thought to himself, I do have lovely parents.

Peter arrived back in his lodgings in Temple Cowley, a suburb of Oxford near the Morris Motors car factory, on the first Sunday of October 1973. He would return to work at the Oxford Mail the following day. Barry and Aline Evans had lived in the small terraced house for nearly forty years, since Barry arrived in Cowley in the 1930s. His story was remarkable, but not that unusual for the time. During the depression he had walked from his birthplace in South Wales to Cowley to find work in the expanding car factory. He found work almost immediately and had escaped from the grinding poverty of his youth. He met Aline, who had arrived in Oxford from County Donegal, Ireland, soon after he had found work in the factory. They married within twelve months and had lived in Temple Cowley ever since. Barry had recently retired and to supplement his pension, they decided to take in a lodger. Peter was their first lodger and the three of them got along famously. Barry and Aline had no children of their own, which had been a great disappointment to them, and had taken Peter under their wing, visiting him in hospital during his stay at the Radcliffe Infirmary and taking an interest in his career as a reporter at the Oxford Mail. Peter would occasionally join them at the Morris Motors Social Club on a Saturday night for chicken in the basket and a couple of pints of beer. It was a happy home.

On the Monday morning at the Oxford Mail's new offices in Osney Mead, Peter was welcomed back to work by the editor, Sidney Newman. Newman was a tough, no nonsense Yorkshireman who had moved to Oxford at the end of the Second World War to work as a reporter. He became editor of the paper in 1962 and was both liked and revered by the staff at the newspaper. It was said that he would never ask a reporter to undertake a task that he wasn't prepared to do himself and although it was never mentioned in the office, it was well known amongst the staff that he had been awarded the Victoria Cross for gallantry in the face of the enemy during the war. He had a close knit team of reporters and ran a tight ship, as they say.

It was typical of Newman to get straight down to business as soon as he had welcomed Peter back and enquired about his health. Newman had decided that he wanted to make one or two changes at the newspaper and this included asking Peter to take on the role of attending Council meetings and reporting directly to him on any political matters that needed covering. The other change he had made was to ask Mathew Phillips-Lehman to look after all University matters for the newspaper. Newman told

Peter that he thought they would make a good partnership reporting on two key areas for the newspaper. The meeting had taken all of ten minutes, which was typical of Sidney Newman, and Peter was soon back at his desk. He recognised these changes as another opportunity to learn his trade and he looked forward to working more closely with Mathew. In a city like Oxford, Council affairs would often overlap with university matters and he had already struck up a good relationship with Mathew. They had known each other whilst they were both studying at Oxford and even though they came from very different backgrounds, they held a mutual respect for each other. Peter had, what was often described as flair when it came to reporting and in his short time working for the newspaper, he had already uncovered a number of interesting stories. Mathew was more of a details man and was scrupulously thorough whenever covering a story. Peter agreed with Sidney Newman, they would make a good team!

Peter soon became engrossed in Oxford City Council matters, reporting on Council meetings and building up relationships with a number of Councillors. It was partly through one of these relationships that Peter would uncover a scandal that would make his name as a local investigative reporter and propel him towards a career with one of the national papers in London. He had become friendly with one of the younger Councillors, Jim Taylor, who sat on the City Council's Planning Committee. Peter would occasionally meet Jim in town for a pint at lunch time. The *Turf Tavern* was their favourite haunt and they would spend a good hour exchanging stories connected with their working lives. Jim had grown up in Oxford, was proud of his City and was always keen to hear about any interesting stories from the newspaper that Peter was prepared to share with him and in exchange, Jim would provide Peter with the odd piece of gossip from the City Council. It was at one of these lunch meetings in '*The Turf*' just before Christmas 1973 that Jim shared an interesting piece of gossip that had been puzzling him. An application had come before the Planning Committee to develop housing in the west of the City.

"The developer's plan is to build up to thirty executive detached houses on the land." Jim explained.

"Nothing odd about that Jim, we could do with more housing, particularly in the west of the City." Peter replied.

"I agree," Jim continued, "but, there are some major obstacles the developer would need to overcome to achieve their objectives. Firstly, a new road link to the Western bypass will be required. Secondly, the proposed route for the new road would result in the demolition of an old people's home and three old farm cottages, which are currently only just about accessible by car up an old lane and finally, the existing planning regulations are very clear, that the land can only be developed in exceptional circumstances."

"Sounds as though the developer should look elsewhere then Jim." Peter suggested.

"Well, I agree, you would have thought so but, what is puzzling me is that Bob Buckle is all for it and seems determined to get the application approved at January's Planning Committee meeting. He's already managed to force it through some of the early planning stages."

"That doesn't sound like Bob at all, in the short time I've known him he's always come across as being a very cautious kind of bloke, a safe pair of hands and anyway, he must be near retirement age?" asked Peter.

"Exactly!" Jim said warming to the subject. "He'll be 65 in March next year and will retire with a full pension and the respect of so many at the Council, he's very popular. He's become a bit of a legend to be honest and has chaired the Planning Committee meetings for more than ten years, but this is totally out of character."

31

"Yes, that is odd, I'll tell you what Jim I'll make a few discrete enquiries." Peter had become interested in Jim's story, "Who's the current owner of the land?"

"University owned, St. Bernard's College." Jim replied.

"And the developer?" Peter asked.

"RSM Property, a London firm."

"Leave it with me Jim and don't worry, I'll be very discrete, another pint? After all, it is nearly Christmas!" Peter smiled.

Peter had been back at work for almost three months now and was feeling guilty that he still hadn't contacted Taraneh. It puzzled him, when he took time to think about it, that he felt quite shy and at times, nervous, when in the company of girls like Taraneh. She was clearly a good, thoughtful, kind person as well as good looking and it was this combination that would make him feel anxious, although he was pretty sure that no one would ever dream he felt these emotions. Outwardly, he gave the impression of being extremely confident, charming and good fun. Oddly enough, during his conversations with Taraneh in hospital he sometimes got the impression that she could see through this facade and somehow, she understood his vulnerabilities. He remembered her looking at him as though she knew exactly what he was really thinking. Another, more practical reason, for him not contacting Taraneh was that he was currently dating a girl called Debbie, who worked for the Council in the Town Hall. He had met her when he was seeing Shirley, they lived near to each other and Debbie would often be in the pub where he and Shirley used to meet on Wednesday evenings. Again, their relationship was what would be described as casual. They would meet a couple of times a week for a drink in town and occasionally a bite to eat afterwards. The difficulty they had was finding somewhere they could be alone together. There was no way he could take her back to his lodgings in Temple Cowley, as kind as Barry and Aline were, they were quite straight-laced! Debbie lived at home with her mum and dad, who seldom went out in the evenings, so opportunities for them to get to know one another were quite rare!

It was Christmas Eve and Peter was going to spend a few days with his parents in Birmingham but, before he caught the train, he bought a Christmas card and a bunch of flowers from the Covered Market in Oxford and walked along St. Giles towards the Radcliffe Infirmary. As he approached Doyle Ward he recognised Sister Jenny Roberts and asked her whether Taraneh was on duty. Sister Roberts remembered Peter and smiled.

"Hello Peter, how is your sight?" she asked

"Good, thanks to Mr. Hawtrey and all the staff here!" Peter laughed.

"Taraneh has a day off today Peter, I'm afraid she drew the short straw and is working tomorrow on Christmas Day." Sister Roberts told him.

"Could I leave this card and flowers for her please Sister?" Peter asked, strangely feeling himself blush.

"Of course you can dear, she'll be delighted I'm sure." Sister Roberts smiled.

As Peter hurried off to the railway station he wondered whether Taraneh would call him on his office number, which he'd written on the card.

Mathew Phillips-Lehman sat waiting for Peter wondering what could be so important that he had felt it necessary to book a room for their meeting. Normally, they would meet at each other's desk and discuss the stories they were working on for the paper. Mathew had first come across Peter whilst they were studying at Oxford. They both rowed and would often bump into each other down by the Thames. On the face of it, they couldn't be more different, Mathew was from a family of wealthy landowners in

33

Surrey, had been educated at Public School before Oxford, was studious and even though he had a bit of a reputation for being a ladies man, quite shy. However, Mathew remembered being told that opposites often attract and he enjoyed Peter's company. They would often share a pint at the University Rowing Club and discuss politics and music, in which they were both interested. They had joined the Oxford Mail on the same day and had recently started meeting for a pint over lunch, when the opportunity arose. Little did either of them realise at the time that they would still be meeting regularly for a lunchtime pint forty years later!

Peter arrived carrying a mug of tea in each hand and clenching a paper bag, containing two Chelsea buns, between his teeth.

"Sorry I'm a bit late Matt, I was waiting for Molly with the tea trolley!" Peter apologised.

"That's jolly decent of you old boy, how much do I owe you?" Mathew asked, whilst thinking to himself and smiling that he'd never known Peter being on time for a meeting, unless it was with the editor Sidney Newman.

"That's alright Matt, my treat, I expect you're wondering what's with all the cloak and dagger stuff, booking an office for our meeting."

"Well, it did cross my mind old boy." Mathew smiled.

Peter told Mathew about his conversation in the *Turf Tavern* with Jim Taylor and asked him whether he knew anything about St. Bernard's College and their plans to sell its land in West Oxford. Mathew listened quietly to what Peter had to say, making the occasional note, whilst enjoying his tea and Chelsea bun. He had assumed the meeting would touch on University business and consequently, had brought along some relevant files with him to the meeting.

"St. Bernard's is a wealthy college Peter and a lot of its assets are tied up in land and property. They have been selling off some land over the past few years to reinvest in the stock markets, but this is unusual."

Just as Peter expected, Mathew was already on top of his brief since Sidney Newman had asked him to take over University matters and importantly, knew the detail.

"You see Peter, colleges in Oxford are usually very reluctant to sell off land so close to the City centre, primarily because they may have uses for it in the future, for example, student accommodation, sports facilities, additional college buildings and so on." Mathew explained.

"Who makes the decision to sell the land?" Peter asked.

"Well that's a very good question Peter, particularly in the case of St. Bernard's. They have a Board of Governors, which will ultimately give approval for the sale of any land or property. However, they also have a very forceful Master at St. Bernard's, Roland Makepiece and interestingly, whilst he may be an authority on ancient Greek literature old boy, he made his fortune as a property developer in London. He chairs a number of influential University committees and from what I've heard, he is the real decision maker at St. Bernard's College. Who is the property developer Peter?" Mathew asked.

"RSM Property, a London firm." Peter replied, impressed by Mathew's grasp of the detail.

Mathew thumbed through the files he had brought along to the meeting.

"That's interesting Peter," Mathew replied calmly, "Roland Makepiece used to sit on RSM's Board as a non-executive Director."

It was a cold day in early January when Peter met Debbie for lunch in the Golden Egg restaurant in George Street. He enjoyed Debbie's company and she often had some gossip from the Town Hall, which came in useful. She was always dressed in the latest fashion, Peter noticed she was wearing a check patterned maxi dress today and she had a

35

mischievous sense of humour, which appealed to him. Debbie had told him, in her usual forthright way, she found him very attractive, particularly his physique which had improved following years of rowing and football training. She even said that she found his Brummie accent cute, which was a first! They both ordered sausage, egg and chips with a mug of tea and Peter asked for a couple of slices of bread and butter as well. No sooner had their meals arrived when Bob Buckle came into the restaurant with another Council Officer. Peter nodded and Bob nodded back, Debbie, being her usual cheeky self, smiled at the Councilor.

"That's twice in two days we've bumped into each other Mr. Buckle, people will start talking if we're not careful!" Debbie joked.

Bob Buckle laughed, but Peter noticed it was a slightly uncomfortable moment for him and he soon disappeared to the far end of the busy restaurant with his companion, where they found a table.

"What was all that about then?" asked Peter when the Councilors were out of earshot.

"Oh, I bumped into him yesterday in East Oxford, he was coming out of Jim Catlin's on the Cowley Road." Debbie replied.

"Jim Catlin's?" Peter looked puzzled.

"Yes, the bookmakers," Debbie explained. "To be honest, I've seen him going in and out of there a few times over the past few months."

"Bob's not an East Oxford man is he Debbie?" Peter asked.

"Oh no! not anymore he's not, he moved up market over five years ago, Cumnor Hill I think," Debbie replied. "Shall we have another cup of tea Peter? I've got some good news to tell you, my mum and dad are going away for the weekend and I'll have the house all to myself!"

"Not just yourself I hope Debbie!" Peter winked and they both laughed.

Peter returned to the office and reflected upon what he had discovered so far. RSM Property, a London firm, was planning to buy a large piece of land in West Oxford to build thirty executive houses. Nothing odd about that, he thought. The land is currently owned by St. Bernard's College, which is not accustomed to selling off land in the City, so close to the college. Unusual. The Master of St. Bernard's, Roland Makepiece, has a previous connection with RSM Property and is influential in any decision making regarding land and property sales for the college. Suspicious. A planning application has been put before the City Council to develop the land in West Oxford, approval of which would result in a new road being built linking the development to the Western Bypass and the demolition of an old people's home and three cottages. Bob Buckle, who retires in less than three months' time, is supporting the application even though the existing planning regulations stipulate that the land can only be developed in exceptional circumstances. Buckle's behaviour is completely out of character and is raising a few eyebrows of other Council officials. Worrying. Buckle has been seen frequenting a bookmakers in East Oxford, which may or, may not, have anything to do with events at the Council.

These were the facts that Peter presented to Sidney Newman during a meeting he had requested with the editor the following Monday morning. Mathew also attended the meeting. Peter knew that Mathew could be relied on to fill in any gaps that he left during his presentation. During a long career in local news, there wasn't much that Sidney Newman had not come across before. He was extremely well respected, not just at the paper but throughout the City and beyond. Newman listened quietly, occasionally asking for clarification of some detail, whilst Peter and Mathew told him about their discovery. When they had finished, he questioned them in detail about the source of their information and the reliability of their contacts. What happened next was typical Sidney Newman. After about an hour, he shuffled the papers in front of him into a tidy pile, stood up behind his desk and looked straight at the young reporters.

"Well done, here's what we're going to do next. Peter, I want you to find out as much as you can about RSM Property. Here's the name and phone number of a contact in London you should speak with." Newman scribbled the details on a piece of paper and handed it to Peter. "He's ex CID and specialised in property development crime, mention my name when you call him. Visit him in London, if necessary. Mathew, more information on Roland Makepiece please, speak with the Bursar at Wakefield College, Donald West, be discrete. I'll speak with Bob Buckle, I've known him for twenty odd years and there may still be time to save his bacon, never mind his pension, before he does something stupid!"

And with that, the meeting was over and Sidney Newman was already making a phone call about another, completely unrelated, news story even before Peter and Mathew had left his office.

CHAPTER SIX

THE SCOOP

Peter got off the train at Paddington Station and walked along Praed Street and on to Craven Road clutching a photocopied page from the London A-Z, which he had brought with him for guidance. It was a bitterly cold, but bright, January morning. He had caught an early train from Oxford Station and as he turned into Gloucester Terrace he was joined by, what he assumed were, office and shop staff making their way to work. He liked the feel and energy of London. He turned on to the Bayswater Road and entered Kensington Gardens through Black Lion Gate. His meeting with Terry Dixon was arranged for 9.30am in the foyer of the *Royal Garden Hotel*, which was located at the end of Kensington High Street. Peter had deliberately chosen to walk, rather than taking the tube, to clear his thoughts ahead of the meeting. He was excited, but also slightly nervous, which he tried to convince himself was normal when investigating an important story.

He needn't have worried, Terry Dixon greeted him warmly on his arrival and ordered tea and toast for them both at the table he had reserved near to the reception area. Terry, who Peter had noticed was well known with the staff at the hotel, must have been in his sixties, but looked fit and well for his age.

"Pity you didn't come at lunch time lad, we could have done this over a couple of pints!" Terry said in a broad Yorkshire accent. "So you work for Sid then Peter, he phoned me yesterday and spoke very highly of you."

Peter was surprised to hear someone calling the editor Sid and smiled, in the office it was either Mr. Newman or, Sidney to those who had known him for a long time. He was also secretly pleased to have been praised by the editor.

"We were at school together me and Sid, back in Yorkshire, aye those were the days lad!" Terry laughed.

Feeling totally at ease, Peter ran through the key points of the story he was working on and asked Terry what he knew about RSM Property.

"Aye, RSM Property or Roland Stanley Makepiece Property to give it its original name." announced Terry, suddenly more serious, "Interesting, they were on our radar for years when I worked for the Met, yet we could never quite pin anything on them, we came close once or twice though. Roland Makepiece setup the company soon after the war and made a fortune redeveloping bomb sites in prime sites in central London, all legitimate as far as we knew. Most people were just pleased to see all the mess from the blitz being cleared up and couldn't really care less whether anyone was making money out of it. Things changed in the early sixties though, he went into partnership with Barry Golding, who owned property in Soho and they started acting as landlords, charging dodgy businesses in the area extortionate rent. Makepiece was keen to protect his ambitions in the academic world though and sold out his share of the business soon after this change of the direction for the company." Terry paused and poured more tea. "Following this, RSM became involved with some highly dubious business dealings, particularly in Soho. We had several run-ins with them throughout the sixties, but never quite had enough evidence to charge anyone. Golding still owns the company and from what I hear on the grapevine, runs it very hands-on."

"Do you think Golding and Makepiece are still in touch Terry?" asked Peter.

"Oh yes, I should think so, Golding's son married Makepiece's daughter and there are grandchildren. The son works for the firm, it's a family business!" Terry chuckled.

Donald West took the short walk from Wakefield College to the *Lamb & Flag* in St. Giles and sat in the back bar, where he knew it would be quiet at lunchtime. He had been the Bursar at Wakefield College for the best part of twenty years and there were few important financial matters affecting the University of which he was unaware. A Glaswegian, West had come to Oxford in the fifties to take up his position as Bursar at Wakefield and it was not long after his arrival that he came across Sidney Newman at the Oxford Mail. West had been wrongly accused of a crime in Oxford and it was largely thanks to an investigation led by Newman for the paper that his name was cleared of any wrong doing and he was able to continue his career at Wakefield College. He was eternally grateful for Newman's intervention and as a way of showing his gratitude, he had provided him with the occasional titbit of news over the years regarding the University, particularly regarding financial matters.

Mathew Philips-Lehman was unaware of this as he introduced himself and asked West whether he would like another drink.

"It's a bit early for me Mathew, but a wee dram would be very nice, *Teachers* please if they've got it." West replied in a broad Glaswegian accent.

Mathew returned with the whisky and a pint of *Double Diamond* for himself.

"Thank you for agreeing to see me Mr. West, I'll try not to take up too much of your time." Mathew began, ever the gentleman. "It concerns the sale of some land in West Oxford owned by St. Bernard's College and Roland Makepiece's involvement with the sale."

41

Donald took a sip of his whisky and looked Mathew in the eye.

"I can assume that this discussion is private and I will not be mentioned in any article which may appear in the paper?" West asked, looking stern.

"You have my word Mr. West." Mathew had sensed some tension the moment Makepiece's name was mentioned.

"The sale of the land in West Oxford has raised eyebrows throughout the University and is seen as a crusade being led by Roland Makepiece. Let me be clear laddie, I have no axe to grind concerning Makepiece, to be honest I've had very little to do with him over the years, the odd University committee meeting or college dinner, but I do have some very reliable contacts at St. Bernard's and they are extremely concerned about this matter. All I will say is that I understand Makepiece's son-in-law has been spending a lot of time at the college and perhaps questions should be asked concerning, shall we say, irregular payments being made between the developer and the Master of St. Bernard's!" and with that, Donald West finished his whisky, stood up and shook hands with Mathew before leaving.

Mathew sat alone for a few minutes following West's dramatic departure and finished his beer. Crikey, it looks as though Peter's on to something he thought to himself!

It was early on Thursday morning and Peter and Mathew were sitting in Sidney Newman's office. Newman, who had called them in for an unscheduled meeting, was on the phone to Basil Bridgewater, the newspaper's lawyer.

"Thank you Basil, I'll be back in touch later today." Newman put the phone down and came straight to the point, "I met with Bob Buckle last night concerning the planning application from RSM Property. Before I update you, I

42

want you both to tell me the details of your meetings with Terry Dixon and Donald West."

Peter and Mathew both referred to their notes whilst they updated the editor. Peter could feel a tension in the room and was careful to ensure he gave an accurate account of his meeting with Terry Dixon. Newman made the odd note whilst they briefed him and now and then asked them to clarify a particular point. When they had both finished, Newman smiled and told them that Buckle had confirmed virtually everything the young reporters had told him. Buckle had been offered £2,000 by Golding's son to ensure that the planning application be approved by the Council.

"Buckle has evidence of the attempted bribe and will be reporting it to the police later today. He told me it was never his intention to accept the bribe and he was just playing Golding along, whilst he made some investigations himself. He had made the connection between Golding and Roland Makepiece as well. He asked me for twenty-four hours before we print any story." Newman told them in his customary, no nonsense style and continued, "So, here's what we're going to do. I want you to work together for the rest of the day and draft a piece on this for tomorrow's lunchtime edition. Peter, I want you to lead on the story, Mathew you're to provide support and check every word that's drafted. I want you both to be credited in the byline. We'll meet at four o'clock this afternoon and I'll review and edit, if necessary, before I run it past Basil." Sidney Newman was already on his feet and checking his watch, which was indication that the meeting was over.

"One more thing before you go," Newman said, "the nationals in Fleet Street will probably be interested in this story, it has all the ingredients they enjoy, apart from sex, let me know immediately if you have any calls from them once it has gone to print!"

43

It was mid-February when Peter's phone rang and Carol, one of the receptionists at the paper, told him that there was a Miss Taraneh Saderzadeh on the line for him. Peter wasn't quite sure why, but he suddenly felt slightly nervous.

"Put her through please Carol." Peter asked.

"Taraneh?"

"Hello Peter, how are you?" Taraneh sounded genuinely pleased to hear his voice.

"I'm well thank you, how is nursing and the Radcliffe Infirmary?"

"Oh, it is good thank you Peter and I have some news I would like to tell you about, could we meet, perhaps for afternoon tea one day this week?" Taraneh asked. "I am on night shift and I usually awake by two in the afternoon."

"How about tomorrow, do you know Maxwell's in town? I could be there at four o'clock." Peter suggested.

"I will see you there tomorrow then Peter."

"I have some news to tell you as well Taraneh, see you tomorrow!"

Peter smiled as he put down the phone.

Peter took his favourite window seat in Maxwell's just before four o'clock and Taraneh joined him shortly afterwards. Peter hadn't seen her for nearly five months, since he was discharged from hospital and had never seen her dressed in anything other than her nurse's uniform. She was dressed casually, but fashionably, in bell-bottom blue denim jeans, platform shoes and under her navy blue coat, a pale blue cheesecloth shirt. After Peter had ordered them tea and scones, with fresh cream and strawberry jam, they both spoke at once trying to apologise for not getting in touch with each other earlier and then laughed.

"You go first Taraneh!" Peter said, still smiling.

"First of all, how are your eyes Peter?" Taraneh asked.

44

"The right one is back to normal thanks and Mr. Hawtrey was right, it seems to compensate for the poor sight in my left eye, I remember him telling me the right eye will work overtime!" Peter laughed. "Crikey, Mr. Hawtrey, he was a character, does he still do his rounds in the mornings?" asked Peter.

"Oh yes, he is a terrible flirt when Matron is not around, Rita told me that she saw him having a drink one evening with Sister Roberts, mind you Rita has some gossip about everyone!" Taraneh laughed. "And your lovely parents, how are they Peter?"

"They are both in good health thanks, it's a pity they're not here you could discuss your news with my father in Farsi!" Peter joked.

They both laughed and Peter felt that slight nervousness he had experienced when she called him on the telephone the day before.

"So, my news Peter," Taraneh announced smiling, "I am engaged to be married!"

It was so unexpected that, for a brief moment, Peter just stared at her open mouthed. However, he quickly composed himself.

"Congratulations Taraneh and who is the lucky man?" he asked.

She told him that his name is David and he is a junior doctor at the Radcliffe. She first met him when she attended a training course back in October last year. She told Peter that, in line with Persian tradition, she had visited her father in London a few weeks ago asking for his agreement to their marriage and the following week he visited them both in Oxford and gave his consent. They would marry in Tehran later in the year. Peter could tell that she was so happy and whilst he felt slightly sad at hearing the news, in truth, he was very pleased for her.

"Will you continue nursing Taraneh?" Peter asked.

"Yes, of course, nursing is my vocation and I will continue as long as I can," she replied, "Now, enough about me, you must tell me about your news Peter. Rita tells me you have become quite famous following your story in the Oxford Mail! She reads it every day in the canteen during her lunch break and keeps me up to date with the local news you know. She remembered you from when you were in hospital and thought you were quite dishy!" Taraneh joked and they both laughed.

"Well, my news is partly as a result of that story," Peter said, "I've been offered a job as a reporter working in Fleet Street for one of the national newspapers and have accepted their offer, I'll move to London next month."

"That is wonderful news Peter, congratulations!" and Taraneh leant across the table and kissed him on both cheeks, "Where will you live?"

"My work colleague and friend, Mathew, has also been offered a job working for the paper and we are planning to share a flat together, in fact, we are going flat hunting this weekend."

"They will miss you at the Oxford Mail Peter." Taraneh said.

"Mr. Newman, the editor, has been very good about it really and told me that he had expected me to make it to Fleet Street sooner rather than later, I've learnt so much from him during my time at the paper." Peter said. "Where will you and David live?"

"Here in Oxford, we are putting down a deposit on a small house in Jericho, it's a bit of a run-down area, but it'll do for the time being," Taraneh replied.

They finished their tea and scones and after Peter had paid the bill, they wished each other good luck for the future. Peter said he would write to her at the hospital when he had settled into a flat in London.

46

The next few weeks passed very quickly for Peter. He cleared his desk at the Oxford Mail and enjoyed a joint leaving party with Mathew at the *Turf Tavern*. Debbie and Jim Taylor attended from the City Council as well as a number of colleagues from the newspaper. He spoke with Debbie at the party and they agreed that they would keep in touch when he moved to London, but deep down, they both knew it was unlikely. Sidney Newman gave a short, but hilarious speech and ended it telling the two young reporters that if they ever get bored with the bright lights of London, they were always welcome back at Osney Mead!

Peter and Mathew found a small two bedroom flat in Notting Hill, a short walk from the tube station, where they would travel to and from work each day. Peter gave notice to Barry and Aline that he would be leaving his lodgings and they looked genuinely sad when he told them. He took them both out for a meal in Town before he left, to thank them for looking after him whilst he was in Oxford. He spent the week before he moved to London with his parents in Birmingham. Stanley had recently retired from the railways and Dorothy was complaining that he was getting under her feet! Stanley was looking forward to the Spring weather, when he could spend more time on his allotment. Peter promised them that, as soon as he had settled into his flat, they must come down to London to visit him. Once again, he reflected on how lucky he was to have such caring, loving parents. Stanley and Dorothy were incredibly proud at what their son had achieved in life so far and he had become to appreciate more and more how much his stable upbringing had helped him.

CHAPTER SEVEN

LONDON – 2013

It was a bright sunny day in early May 2013 when Mathew Phillips-Lehman entered *The Elephant and Castle* and ordered two pints of bitter. He asked the young barman to take for both pints, but only pour one of them, he knew Peter would be a few minutes late. Mathew sat at their favourite table facing the door, lifted his iPad out of his shoulder bag, logged in, checked that the pub's Wi-Fi was working and proceeded to look through his emails. He was momentarily distracted by a BBC breaking-news story, regarding the coalition government, which had popped up.

It had been twelve months since Gloria had died and whilst Peter's timekeeping had never been particularly good, to say the least thought Mathew, it had got even worse since his wife's sudden death. Mathew stopped reading his emails for a few moments and thought about his old friend. Two years before Gloria's death, Peter had gone freelance and Mathew had never known him so happy. He would still write the occasional article on defence matters and had started working on a novel, which clearly excited him. He spent more time travelling, both at home and abroad, with Gloria and would enjoy telling him about the trips during their monthly lunch meetings at *The Elephant and Castle*. He had more time to indulge their shared love of live music, which they had kept up for forty odd years, and Mathew fondly remembered a trip to Miami they made in early 2012 with Gloria and one of her friends to see Radiohead. It was the last gig he would attend with Gloria. Since her death, Peter had become quiet and subdued, which was completely out of character. He had stopped writing and freely admitted that, at times, he drank too much. He rarely ventured out of the Victorian terraced house in Marylebone, which he had lovingly cared for with Gloria for the best part of thirty years. Mathew remembered the wonderful dinner parties at the house, when Gloria cooked paella using her Spanish mother's recipe. Gloria would tease him over his very English dress sense, tweed jacket, cavalry twill trousers, Oxford brogues and of course, the number of different girlfriends he had arrived with over the years. "Mathew's lady friends," was how Peter always jokingly described them! It was ironic and a long running joke between the three of them that it was Mathew, the quiet, sensible, conservative minded details man, who had the turbulent love life, whilst it was the more fashionably dressed, modern minded Peter, who had been happily married for thirty years.

Peter Wilson looked at his watch as he left High Street Kensington underground station and crossed the road. He wound his way up Kensington Church Walk, hearing the lovely sound of the children in the playground of *St Mary Abbots Primary School*. Lunch time he thought. At the top, he turned left on Holland Street and then through the front door of *The Elephant and Castle*. How many times had he done that he thought to himself. He spotted Mathew immediately, he was sat staring at his iPad.

"Sorry I'm a bit late Matt, bloody Circle Line!" he apologised.

"No problem old boy, your pint's in the stable." Mathew replied cheerfully.

Mathew studied his old friend whilst he was waiting at the bar for his pint to be pulled. He still wore his hair long, although it was grey now and he dressed fashionably for a sixty-three year old, lots of *Paul Smith* and *Armani* thought Mathew he smiled to himself. He had lost weight since

Gloria died. He was always slim, but he looked skinny now and could do with putting on a stone in weight.

"Cheers old boy!" and they clinked glasses as Peter took his seat, "You'll be pleased to hear that the steak and ale pie is back on, I've already ordered if that's alright with you?" Mathew asked him.

"That's good news, I haven't been shopping for a few days and the fridge is bare at home." Peter sighed.

Mathew was just about to tell him he must eat properly when Peter interrupted him.

"Matt, please stop worrying about me, I'll be fine it's just....well, it's just taking a bit longer than I thought it would, you know the grieving."

Mathew felt terribly sorry for his old friend, but thought to himself there was no point in waiting for the right moment, he would dive straight in with his news.

"I had a call from Tricia yesterday Peter." Mathew noticed that Peter looked puzzled, "Do you remember her? Barry Wagstaffe's secretary in the old days at the paper."

"Oh yes, of course, we were all scared of her!" Peter laughed.

"Well she couldn't have been that scary old boy, I seem to remember I took her out once or twice! Anyway, they've arranged a dinner for Barry in recognition of his services to journalism, black tie affair at *The Savoy*, I've got my invitation, have you received yours?" asked Mathew.

"Possibly, I haven't opened my post for over a week." Peter groaned. "So, why did Tricia ring you?"

"Apparently, Barry really wants us both to attend and asked Tricia to make sure we do. It's a three line whip old boy!" Mathew continued, "seriously though, we should both make the effort and go, after all, Barry offered us our first jobs in Fleet Street, it's nearly forty years ago you know."

Peter sat quietly for a few moments deep in thought. He was thinking that he rarely ventured out since Gloria died and when he did, it was either to meet Mathew, with whom he felt totally comfortable or, to the local Waitrose on Marylebone High Street.

"When is it?" Peter asked.

"A week on Friday, I'll order a cab and pick you up on the way if you like, about seven o'clock?"

"Thanks Matt, I'd like that, God only knows where my dinner jacket is, in the attic I expect!"

"Good man! Barry will be delighted, I'm sure there'll be a few other old faces from the past there as well." Mathew smiled at his old friend.

"Yes, that's what's worrying me!" Peter joked.

Peter joined Mathew in the back of the black cab, which set off on its journey to The Strand. Mathew smiled to himself, noticing that Peter clearly felt uncomfortable wearing a dinner jacket, whereas he felt totally at home wearing one. The two of them had known each other for so long, there were times when they almost knew what each other was thinking.

"I see you've been up in the attic then old boy, very smart." Mathew remarked.

Peter smiled, "yes, two hours I spent up there yesterday, whilst I was up there I found some of the articles Gloria wrote during the 1980s for the Sunday supplements, mainly interviews with politicians, they were very good."

"She was a very good writer Peter, a good judge of character I would say, did you find it helped at all?" Mathew asked.

"Yes, it did a bit, I was quite surprised, made me laugh at times," Peter paused and then changed the subject, "so, dinner at *The Savoy*, quite a treat!"

The dinner and speeches had been a great success. A former Foreign Secretary had spoken generously about Barry Wagstaffe, describing him as one of Fleet Street's

.

finest editors. There were about a dozen large dinner tables, each seating ten guests and Peter had been sandwiched between a young Tory MP and a glamourous French journalist, who was based in London working for her newspaper. He noticed, with some amusement, that Mathew had been placed, on another table, next to Tricia! Whilst coffee was being served, it crossed Peter's mind that years ago, cigars would have been lit about this time in the proceedings and he noticed a few guests heading outside for a smoke. It was whilst he was in conversation over coffee with the young Tory MP, who was pleasant enough and certainly enthusiastic, that a distinguished looking man approached them. Peter recognised him immediately. The young MP quickly rose to his feet and addressed him.

"Sir, Robert, good to see you, are you enjoying the evening?"

"Indeed I am." Sir Robert replied looking at Peter.

"Excuse my manners Sir Robert, may I introduce you to Peter Wilson......"

Before the young MP had finished the sentence, Sir Robert smiled, "Good evening Peter, lovely to see you again, must be nearly thirty years."

"Hello Bob." Peter smiled and they shook hands.

"I'm so sorry, I didn't realise you two are already acquainted." the young MP stammered and realising that he was probably no longer required, made his excuses and disappeared.

"Christ! I can't remember the last time I was called Bob, no don't apologise Peter, I quite enjoyed the look on the young lad's face," joked Sir Robert, "and you still haven't lost that Brummie accent I see!"

They both laughed.

"It was you I came over to see actually Peter, about two things really, first of all I wanted to say how sorry I was to hear about your wife, she interviewed me once you know for one of the Sunday magazines, lovely lady, she was excellent."

"Thank you, you sent flowers, that was very kind and I should have written to thank you." Peter looked sad.

"On a brighter note", Sir Robert continued, "I've come over to ask for your help, well your memory really I suppose. This probably sounds terribly pompous, but I'm writing my memoirs, I know I never held any of the highest offices of state, but I was involved, often behind the scenes, during some interesting times and I have a story to tell."

"I'm sure you have and I don't think it's pompous at all Bob." Peter replied and he meant it, he'd always found Bob Coleville straightforward, quite unusual for a politician. He remembered him having that easy charm that some wealthy, successful, handsome men of his generation have. Peter thought how he's often now described as a Tory grandee in the media, a ridiculous term. Peter also noted that he'd lost none of his charm. More interestingly though, he had always felt that beneath the suave exterior there was another, altogether, different character who could be self-depreciating and could recognise some of the absurdities of the world in which he lived.

"I wondered whether you would help me with a part of the book that, to be honest, I'm struggling with and I guess it'll come as no surprise to you Peter that it concerns the scandal at the MOD in the mid-eighties. After all, it was your story for the paper that disclosed the corruption. Look, let's not discuss it now, wrong time and place, but if you're interested give me a ring on this number," and Sir Robert handed Peter his card. "We could talk over lunch I'd enjoy that, my treat, let me know."

Peter ended the evening enjoying a scotch with Mathew in a pub, just off The Strand. He felt more relaxed than he had for a long, long time.

CHAPTER EIGHT

THE PHOTOGRAPH

Margaret Coleville sat waiting in the arrivals lounge for the incoming flight from Stansted to land at Ancona airport. She had risen early at their farmhouse, changed the sheets in the second bedroom and then driven to the airport, ahead of Simon, Patricia and Emily's arrival. She had also checked, for the umpteenth time, that the cot in the small nursery was made up. It was her granddaughter, Emily's first visit to Italy and she wanted it to be perfect for her. It was particularly warm for early May in Le Marche and Maurizio, their neighbour and the local handyman, had already ensured that the swimming pool was ready to use. Simon was a strong swimmer and enjoyed a dip every morning whenever he stayed with his mother at the farmhouse, near the beautiful town of Jesi. Since she had retired, Margaret found herself spending more and more time in Italy and looked forward to Simon and Patricia visiting, particularly now that Emily would be coming with them. Simon had turned forty earlier in the year and becoming a father had been an unexpected surprise for him and Patricia, who had also just turned forty. They had all but given up thinking about having children and although the two of them had been very happy together on their own, the arrival of Emily had delighted them. Margaret and her husband Robert were also delighted and doted on their first grandchild. Robert would join Margaret at the farmhouse for a fortnight in June, she knew just how busy he was at present writing his memoirs and that he preferred to write in London.

54

The journey from the airport to the farmhouse took just under an hour. Simon sat in the front of the Range Rover with his mother, who drove. Although now seventy, she had kept her slim figure and good looks and people were often surprised when she introduced Simon as her son. He had not aged particularly well and looked older than forty. Simon was fond of the good life, drinking and eating a bit too much and he had started to put on the pounds, particularly since Emily was born. Simon and Patricia had met through work, he ran a successful catering business and she often used his company to provide the food and drink at the corporate events, which her company managed. Patricia had decided to take a year off work when Emily was born and was thoroughly enjoying her, somewhat unexpected, role as a mother. In a slightly unusual move, Simon and Patricia had bought his parents' home in Hampstead when they found out that Emily was coming along. It would give them the extra space they wanted and they were also keen that the house should stay in the family. Robert and Margaret had recently moved across London to a smaller, but beautifully appointed property just off the King's Road in Chelsea. They jokingly called it downsizing!

Peter had agreed to meet Sir Robert Coleville for lunch at *L'Escargot,* the French restaurant on Greek Street in Soho. Peter spotted him sat at the table by the window, as he climbed the steps to the restaurant. Peter had dressed casually, but fashionably, Sir Robert was wearing, what looked like, a very expensive pin stripe suit, which made Peter wonder whether he was always so immaculately dressed! He certainly had been whenever their paths crossed in the 1980's, he was well known in political circles then for his sartorial elegance.

"Peter, thank you so much for coming, can I get you a drink before we order?" asked Sir Robert.

Peter asked for a glass of beer and Sir Robert ordered a gin and tonic. After they had ordered lunch, Sir Robert got down to business.

"There's a chapter in the book concerning the Ambrose affair in eighty-four and my personal notes on it are very sketchy," Sir Robert told him. "I remember, at the time, we were told by the security services to be very careful what we said about the affair and not to put anything down on paper. I know it's nearly thirty years ago, but my lawyer has advised me that I'll still have to run this part of the memoirs past the authorities before it's published. It's hardly surprising I suppose, after all, Ambrose had been taking massive personal backhanders for authorising lucrative defence contracts in the Middle East. You broke the story Peter and I just wondered whether you could help me with some of the background and any details on the affair, it must have taken up a great deal of your time back in the day I would imagine?"

"Nearly six months Bob, a lot of the time spent with the paper's lawyers, it's not every day that you discover the Secretary of State for Defence is crooked." Peter replied

"He was a bloody fool, nearly brought down the government. Ironically, his loss was my gain I suppose, the PM asked me to work much more closely with the incoming minister and it eventually led to me getting promoted and a move to the Treasury," Sir Robert smiled. "When your story broke about Sir Stephen Ambrose's gambling debts and the call girls and so on we couldn't believe it you know, he was the most unlikely chap you could ever imagine to get caught up in that sort of business, just shows you how much you really know about other people's private lives."

"I've kept files on most of the major stories I worked on and I'm sure this one will be amongst them, let me have a look and if I do have them, I'll make some notes that you can work from. There may be one or two things that I don't want to include, but I guess you'd expect that." Peter raised his eyebrows.

"Of course Peter, completely understand, but don't hold back on any grizzly details about me, I'm quite thick skinned you know! Look, I'd be happy to provide any remuneration for the work, just let me know how much." Sir Robert offered.

"I don't want paying for the work Bob, it'll keep me busy for a week or so, which is just what I need right now." Peter replied, looking slightly sad.

"That's generous of you Peter," and Sir Robert looked him in the eye, "by the way, for what it's worth, at the time in the MOD we thought you were very good, you didn't try and score any political points, it was just good investigative journalism."

It took Peter more than a week, which involved a number of visits to the attic, to put together the notes on the Ambrose affair, which he had promised Sir Robert Coleville. He found the task stimulating and realised how much he missed his work, particularly the investigative aspects of the job. He had one more meeting with Sir Robert at his club in St James, where he handed over the notes he had prepared. Sir Robert thanked him profusely for his help and promised Peter that he would hear from him when he had finished the book.

The following day, Peter met Mathew at The Elephant and Castle for lunch and Mathew detected a distinct lift in his old friend's mood. Peter told him about the work he'd been doing for Coleville and how much he had enjoyed the task. Mathew teased him about not charging a fee!

"I remember you working on that story, it must have been 1984, I was dating Brenda from the typing pool at the time," Mathew reminisced smiling, "it was quite intense, the fling with Brenda I mean, barely saw you for months, great story though old boy!"

Peter laughed and ordered them both another a pint.

It was a lovely warm early June day and Sir Robert Coleville decided to walk from his home in Chelsea to Sloane Square, where he would take the tube to Bayswater. He would be joining Margaret in Le Marche later in the week. He felt very relaxed, the book was coming along well and the notes that Peter Wilson provided him with were proving particularly helpful. It was the chapter concerning the Ambrose affair that he had been struggling with the most and he was grateful for Peter's help. He would finish the current draft of the book and send it over to the publishers for editing, before leaving for Italy. Whilst he felt a sense of relief, writing his memoirs had left him with some mixed emotions, it had brought back some wonderful memories, but had also reminded him of some very dark moments during his life.

Entering the smart apartment block near Bayswater underground station, Robert nodded to the porter in reception, before taking the lift to the third floor. Julia was waiting for him at the door, she must have seen him crossing the road from the lounge window Robert thought and he smiled as he followed her into the hallway. They embraced affectionately, recently Robert had felt tears welling up whenever they hugged each other. For the best past of forty years Julia had provided a refuge for him, shelter from the storm he sometimes thought to himself, and she had demanded nothing from him, just his love and company. Julia was approaching sixty, but looked ten years younger, slim with shoulder length blonde hair and blue eyes.

"Come through to the kitchen love, I've just put the kettle on." Julia called whilst Robert hung up his jacket in the hallway.

"How are you Julia?" Robert asked taking a seat in the modern kitchen.

"I'm good thanks love, went to the gym this morning for a swim and you, finished that book yet?"

"Nearly, sending a draft to the publisher before I leave for Italy, Margaret's already over there." Robert replied.

"She's happy there on her own?" Julia asked pouring two cups of tea.

"Yes, she says she enjoys her own company these days, mind you, Simon, Patricia and Emily have only just arrived back in Hampstead, so I expect she's had her hands full for a while."

"Oh, of course, grandfather Robert!" Julia teased him.

"Indeed," and Robert laughed, "that reminds me, how's that boy of yours, running the bank yet?"

"He's hardly a boy Robert, he phoned me from New York last night, the Board has asked him to manage the takeover of some small American bank, so he'll be over there for a while I would imagine." Julia told him.

"No sign of any grandchildren for you yet then Julia!" Robert joked.

"He always says he's too busy with his career, he'll have to get his skates on though, he turned forty this year you know."

"Yes, I know he did." Robert said quietly.

It was nearly five o'clock when Robert awoke, he must have dozed off he thought as he stretched. Julia was still asleep next to him and he kissed her forehead. She opened her eyes and smiled at him.

"Will you be staying for dinner?" she asked.

"I'd love to Julia, thank you." Robert replied.

It was late November when the invitation, along with a hand written note, landed on Peter Wilson's door mat. To thank him for his help with the book, Robert and Margaret Coleville would like to invite him to dinner. The hand written note told him there would be about a dozen guests and because of the numbers involved, the dinner would be held at his son's house in Hampstead. Peter remembered Robert telling him that he had recently sold the family home in Hampstead to his son and daughter-in-law. Robert's note was kind, asking after Peter's health and telling him that his publisher had completed the editing and the book would soon be going to print. Peter was relieved to see that the dress code for the evening was casual!

Peter told Mathew about the invitation over lunch at *The Elephant and Castle*. Mathew noted that Peter's mood was continuing to improve, one obvious sign was that he was now opening his post more regularly! Peter told him that he had been asked to prepare a series of articles for one of the broadsheets on the UK's current defence capabilities and had even been interviewed on Radio 4 about the Government's defence export responsibilities. Mathew thought to himself, it was as if a cloud hanging over Peter's head had been lifted and wondered whether the dinner at *The Savoy* and his meeting with Robert Coleville had been a contributory factor. He definitely seemed more relaxed when he had spoken in the back of the cab on the way to the dinner about finding Gloria's articles in his attic. Perhaps reading them had helped him, Mathew certainly hoped so. Over the years, Gloria had occasionally confided in him when she had been concerned about Peter, perhaps when she thought he was working too hard or drinking too much and it was these discussions that, more than anything else, had convinced Mathew just how well she knew Peter and how close they had become. It was hardly surprising that her death had affected him so badly Mathew thought.

"So, when's the big night in Hampstead old boy?" asked Mathew cheerfully.

"Tomorrow night, not sure what to expect really," Peter replied, "another pint Matt?"

Peter took the short walk from his house to Marylebone High Street and hailed a cab. He arrived at Simon

60

Coleville's house in Hampstead in good time for the dinner party. Robert welcomed him warmly and introduced him to his wife Margaret in the drawing room, where the three of them had a glass of champagne. Peter noticed that caterers had been hired for the evening, presumably to allow the hosts to spend more time with their guests. They were soon joined by Simon and his wife Patricia and Peter couldn't help noticing Simon's shock of blonde curly hair, which was just starting to turn grey at his temples. Patricia was a friendly looking woman with a warm smile and it was clear from the outset that the two of them were very comfortable and happy in their new home. Peter asked how their baby daughter Emily was getting on and Patricia told him that she was doing well and was asleep upstairs in the nursery. The other guests soon arrived, they included Robert's publisher and one of the editors of his memoirs. It was a friendly relaxed atmosphere and Robert was a good host, self-effacing and happy to share a joke with his guests. There were no place names on the table when they all went into the dining room, but Margaret had already thought through the seating plan and directed the guests to their seats. Robert was sat at one end of the table and Margaret at the other end, Peter was sat between Patricia and an attractive Spanish lady, who also happened to be a journalist, based in London, working for a Spanish television company. It crossed Peter's mind that, perhaps, he had been deliberately sat next to her! Robert made a short informal speech, thanking everyone around the table, who apparently had all played a part in helping him to complete his memoirs. He told an amusing, slightly exaggerated, story about Peter's role as a brilliant investigative journalist who nearly brought down the Government back in the nineteen-eighties! The food was excellent, shank of lamb for the main course, accompanied by, what Peter thought tasted like, a very expensive French wine.

By the time desert was served there was a very relaxed atmosphere around the table, no doubt helped by the generous amount of wine being consumed. Robert was enjoying himself telling his guests how strange it was coming back to the house that he and Margaret had lived in for more than forty years, as a guest!

"You're hardly a guest father, anyway you've left half of your junk here for me and Pat to clear up!" Simon joked.

Sir Robert laughed, "You're not far wrong Simon, when we came in here for dinner I noticed those old family photographs on the credenza, I said to Margaret before we sat down that I can't believe we forgot to take them with us!"

"Well, if you had left me to organise all the packing Robert we wouldn't have forgotten them," Margaret joined in with a wry smile and added, "Anyway, most of the photographs have Simon in them and I think it would be nice to leave them here now that it's Simon and Pat's home."

Peter and the other guests on his side of the table had turned around during the conversation to get a better look of the photographs on the beautiful French credenza. There were three or four, tastefully framed, family photos and Peter noticed that Margaret was correct, nearly all of them did feature a young Simon. There was one picture amongst them that suddenly caught Peter's attention though. It looked as if it had been taken in the drawing room in colour, but over the years had subsequently faded and the images almost looked as though they were in monochrome. By the look of Robert's flared trousers and matching shirt and tie, as well as Margaret's maxi dress, he thought it was probably taken sometime in the early nineteen-seventies. Sir Robert and Margaret were stood in the forefront of the photograph, but the image that caught his attention was the girl standing in the background lovingly holding a new born baby. Peter was in no doubt of her identity, it was Taraneh Saderzadeh!

Looking back on events later that evening, Peter was surprised and even pleased, at how quickly he had recognised Taraneh Saderzadeh from the photograph and then remembered the unsettling story she had told him forty years earlier, about her time working as a nanny for a wealthy young couple in Hampstead. He was also pleased at his reaction when Sir Robert suggested that they all move to the drawing room, where coffee and liqueurs would be served. He made sure that he was the last guest to leave the dining room and before leaving, deliberately left his mobile phone on the dining table. Whilst coffee was being served in the drawing room and Sir Robert was offering his guests a liqueur, Peter shook his head, cursed his forgetfulness and excused himself, saying he'd just pop back to the dining room to look for his phone. He had left the phone with the camera page open and on returning to the empty dining room, he quickly picked it up from the table where he had left it and took a picture of the framed photograph on the credenza of the Coleville's and Taraneh Saderzadeh. Just as he was slipping the phone back into the inside pocket of his jacket, Margaret Coleville came into the dining room. Peter innocently continued to look at the family photographs.

"You found your phone I hope Peter?" Margaret asked.

"Yes, thank you Margaret, I find I'm getting more and more forgetful these days." Peter lied.

"Robert told me about your wife," Margaret suddenly said, "I'm very sorry, it must have been terrible for you."

"Thank you, it hasn't been easy….I've been admiring your photographs." Peter said, changing the subject.

"Yes, I noticed you looking at them closely before we left for coffee." Margaret paused and Peter got the impression she was studying him for a moment, before she pointed at the photograph with the nanny. "It was taken in 1973, Simon was less than a week old I think, we employed

63

a nanny to help us get over the shock of having a new born baby in the house! Tara, yes Tara, that's what we called her, pretty girl, Persian I seem to remember. I often wonder what became of her, she wanted to be a nurse you know. Shall we go back and join the other guests?"

On his way back to Marylebone in the taxi, Peter thought about the dramatic end to the evening and particularly the conversation with Margaret in the dining room. He got the impression from her behaviour that she knew that he had discovered some secret about her and her family and strangely, wanted to let him know that she knew.

CHAPTER NINE

TEAM WORK

"Did I ever tell you the story about the Persian nurse and the wealthy young Tory MP?" Peter asked.

"No you didn't, but I like the sound of it old boy!" Mathew replied.

It was the week before Christmas and the *Elephant and Castle* was full of local office workers enjoying a few lunch time drinks. Whilst it was a bitterly cold day, the sun was shining and many of the revelers were in the pub's small front garden and a few had even spilled on to Holland Street. Peter and Mathew had found a quieter spot at the back of the pub and were enjoying pints of bitter and cottage pie.

"Taraneh Saderzadeh nursed me in the Radcliffe Infirmary following my car accident, just after we started working at the Oxford Mail do you remember?" Peter recalled.

"I remember it, nasty business, we were all worried about you. Sidney Newman was very concerned, you were on a work assignment when it happened and he felt a bit responsible I think, typical Newman, he contacted the hospital every few days to see if you were alright and made sure you had lots of visitors from the paper."

"Really? You never told me that before." Peter was genuinely surprised and quite touched, Sidney Newman was one of their heroes and his name often cropped up. "Anyway, before becoming a nurse, Taraneh had been working as a nanny in Hampstead for a young couple and their new born baby."

Peter then retold the story that Taraneh had told him forty years ago about the evening she was woken by a violent argument between the young couple, which gave her the impression that, somehow, they had taken home the wrong baby from the maternity hospital.

"Well, to cut a long story short," Peter continued, "I have discovered that she was the nanny for Sir Robert and Margaret Coleville's child, Simon, all those years ago and it was them that she had overheard arguing that night."

"Crikey!" exclaimed Mathew, "It's certainly a remarkable story old boy and do you know what has happened to baby Simon?"

"Simon is forty years old and was at the dinner party last week, in fact, it was held in his house in Hampstead, he recently bought it from his parents and I was sat next to his wife Patricia." Peter replied.

"And you have a feeling that Simon is not really their son, because Margaret Coleville left the maternity hospital in 1973 with another mother's baby?" asked Mathew.

"I know that not all children resemble their parents Matt, but Simon looks nothing like either parent, he has pale skin, blonde hair and blue eyes, whereas Robert had dark hair when he was younger, of course he's gone grey now and Margaret also had dark hair and they both have brown eyes." Peter took out his phone and showed Mathew the photograph he had taken in the dining room. "And, there is something else Matt, it's purely a gut feeling, Margaret spoke to me when we were alone in the dining room after I had discretely taken a picture of the photograph and I got the distinct impression that she knew that I was suspicious about something."

"So, if Simon is not their real son, what happened to the child that Margaret gave birth to in 1973?" asked Mathew.

"A good question Matt and I've decided to try and find out the answer."

Mathew hadn't seen his old friend so animated for a long time, certainly not since Gloria's death.

"I have found out," Peter continued, "that Simon was born on the 15th of January 1973, it wasn't difficult to find this out, he is a director of his own catering company and there is so much company information available on the internet it was quite straightforward, the date also corresponds with information about Sir Robert Coleville on the web."

"Do you know where Simon was born Peter?" Mathew asked.

"No I don't, but at the time of the birth, Robert and Margaret were living in the house in Hampstead where I had dinner last week, so I suppose there's a good chance that Margaret would have been in the local maternity hospital, wherever that was for people living in Hampstead at that time." Peter replied.

"So, find out the hospital where Margaret Coleville gave birth on the 15th January 1973 and the names of the other mothers who gave birth there around that time," Mathew suggested.

"Of course, Margaret's birth-child could have died in the hospital or was sick perhaps, which may explain why she took home someone else's child."

"Possibly, we'll never know though unless we make some enquiries." Mathew added.

"I notice you're using the term 'we' Matt, does that signify that we're going to be working as a team again?" asked Peter smiling and Mathew laughed.

"Well, finding a mother who gave birth to a child forty years ago is not going to be easy and just supposing you do find her and possibly the child that she left the maternity hospital with, what are you planning to do then?" Mathew asked.

"I haven't thought that through yet Matt, mind you, supposing Simon's real mother is alive, she could be anything from between fifty-five and eighty-five years old!" Peter replied.

"Why don't you leave this with me for a few days Peter, I've still got some contacts who probably know how to find out this kind of information, where to look and who to speak with and so on."

Peter remembered that throughout his career Mathew had built up a broad spectrum of contacts and there were some of them that he really didn't want to know about!

"Have you got anything planned for Christmas Peter? You know you're welcome to come down to Surrey with me, all the family will be there and they'd love to see you."

"That's so kind of you Matt, when are you going down there?"

"I'll be travelling down on Christmas Eve and coming back the day after Boxing Day, what do you think?"

"I'd love to come, thank you, I'm glad you're not going earlier that's all, I've got a date on Sunday night!" Peter waited for Mathew's reaction.

"That's good news old boy, anyone I know?" asked Mathew smiling.

"Isabella Dolores Ruiz, she's a journalist based in London, working for a Spanish TV company." Peter announced.

"She's not a Brummie then!" Mathew said in his best Birmingham accent and they both laughed.

CHAPTER TEN

CHRISTMAS 2013

Sir Robert and Margaret Coleville arrived in Hampstead on Christmas Eve laden with gifts. They had driven from Chelsea that morning and Simon and Patricia helped them inside with the presents. It was to be Emily's first Christmas and the family had pulled out all the stops to make it memorable, even though she was too little to understand what was happening! Patricia's parents would be arriving on Christmas Day for lunch and Patricia and Margaret had agreed to share the cooking, which included turkey and all the trimmings. Margaret would be flying off to the farmhouse in Italy the day after Boxing Day, where she would spend the New Year with some old girl friends she had first met when working as a scientist, nearly forty years ago. Later on in the evening, Robert and Simon walked around to the local pub, whilst Margaret and Patricia put some final touches to the decorations in the dining room, ahead of tomorrow's Christmas lunch.

"I thought the dinner to celebrate Robert finishing his book went well last week Margaret." Patricia said, whilst standing on a step ladder hanging up a retro paper chain.

"Yes, it was kind of you and Simon to host the dinner Pat, I like the new place in Chelsea but there's not enough room for entertaining on that scale." Margaret said.

"I could see Isabella getting on like a house on fire with the journalist chap, what was his name?" Patricia asked.

"Peter Wilson," replied Margaret, "he's a good looking chap, they suit each other, he's from Robert's past you know, an authority on defence matters and in those days, he also had a great reputation as an investigative journalist. His wife died suddenly just over a year ago, terrible. Robert really likes him, says he's the most down to earth person he's ever met!"

"Well, he certainly impressed Isabella, she popped in for a coffee the morning after the dinner party and told me they would be meeting again perhaps there is romance in the air!" Patricia laughed, she had her back to Margaret and didn't hear any response, so turned around to see that she was deep in thought.

"After dinner, I caught him looking closely at the photographs on the credenza." Margaret said, pointing at them.

"He left his phone in here or something didn't he and came back to look for it?"

"Mmmm…so he said," Margaret mumbled, "shall we decorate the credenza as well Pat?"

The pub was full with people celebrating Christmas early when Robert and Simon arrived. They had managed to find two seats at the bar and were discussing Simon's catering business, in which Robert had always taken a great interest.

"You've done well with that business Simon, I'm very proud of you, do you still cook much yourself?" Robert asked.

"Not as much as I would like, just don't find the time, too much paper work, although Pat is a great help with it now she has some time on her hands when Emily's asleep."

The two of them were suddenly interrupted by a familiar Spanish accent directly behind them." Hello you two, out boozing while the wives are at home cooking!" Isabella laughed.

"Isabella! How lovely to see you!" Robert greeted her with a kiss on both cheeks.

"Can I get you a drink Isabella?" Simon asked.

"Thank you so much Simon, but I'm with some friends in the other bar, I spotted you when I went to the loo. I just wanted to thank you both for inviting me to the lovely dinner party last week and particularly for sitting me next to Peter!" she smiled.

"You're very welcome," Robert replied, "but I'm afraid neither of us can take the credit for the seating arrangements, that was all down to Margaret!"

"I hear you've been out for a romantic dinner with Peter since then Isabella." Simon teased her.

"Yes, on Sunday, he took me to a lovely restaurant and I had a wonderful time, I just hope Peter did as well, I'm sure he thinks I talk too much, afterwards I realised that I'd spoken about myself a lot, but didn't find out much about him! You said at the dinner party that he was a very good journalist Robert, we just didn't find time to talk about work."

"I have a lot of respect for him Isabella," Robert cut in, "he worked with a small team of investigative journalists years ago, Phillips-Lehman worked with him in those days, terrific partnership, they won awards, he certainly kept us in the Government on our toes, I can tell you!"

"And handsome as well!" Isabella laughed, "Happy Christmas!"

Peter had dressed in a navy blue *Paul Smith* suit, open necked white shirt and a pair of dark brown tasseled loafers for his dinner date with Isabella. He felt slightly nervous as he hailed the cab and asked the driver to take him to Piccadilly Circus. His nervousness certainly wasn't caused by the prospect of long awkward silences over dinner, Isabella had plenty to say in Hampstead last week, she had hardly drawn breath! Thinking about it in the taxi, he realised that it was the first time he'd been out with a woman since Gloria passed away and it was hardly surprising if he was a bit anxious, for a number of reasons.

71

He needn't have worried, because when Isabella arrived at the *Criterian Restaurant* she carried on where she had left off the previous week. She was fascinated when Peter told her about the history of the Neo-Byzantine style restaurant, his favourite eating place in London, from being used as a meeting place for Women's suffrage in the early twentieth century, as a set in numerous movies and even being converted to become *Boots*, the chemist, for a few years after the Second World War.

"It's a beautiful restaurant Peter, thank you so much for bringing me here, look at the ceiling its fantastic!" Isabella said enthusiastically.

Isabella asked him about his wife and Peter felt comfortable telling her about their relationship and the shock of her sudden death and how he had taken a long time to come to terms with the loss. She told him about her early life in Spain, a failed marriage and her move to London five years ago, when she settled in Hampstead.

"Robert and Margaret have been kind neighbours and I will miss them now they've moved to Chelsea, although I was so happy when they told me that Simon and Pat would be moving in, Pat has become a good friend." Isabella told Peter.

The evening was a success and as Peter hailed a cab for her, they joked that they hadn't spoke about work all night, quite an achievement for two journalists! They agreed that Peter would call her after Christmas.

On Christmas Eve, Peter took a cab to Mathew's flat in Kensington. Mathew would drive them down to his family's home near Guildford in Surrey. On the drive down they discussed families and Mathew agreed with Peter that, at sixty-three, he was extremely lucky to have both parents still alive and living in their own home. Mathew's parents were both now ninety years old and whilst they had recently started to look quite frail, they were still fairly active.

Mathew's sister Judith and her husband Colin shared the house with them and their two sons Archie and Tom, who both worked and lived in London, had already joined them at home for Christmas. Mathew's older brother, John, would be joining them on Christmas morning. John, who had spent his working life in the Police Force, rising to the rank of Chief Inspector, was now retired and lived alone in Scotland. Sat in five acres of land, the Victorian property looked impressive in the winter sunshine as they drove up the gravel drive.

Peter had met Mathew's family many times beforehand and was warmly welcomed to their home. As Peter greeted Mathew's parents, he remembered them attending his wedding to Gloria more than thirty years ago, in fact, Mathew's father struck up an unlikely friendship with Stanley, Peter's father at the wedding. Peter had thought at the time that a stockbroker and a railway man may not have much in common, but it was the railways that provided the link. Stanley had worked on the railways all his adult life and Mathew's father, was a railway enthusiast. Following Peter's wedding, the two of them wrote to each other regularly and occasionally met at steam railway conventions until Stanley passed away in 1995.

It was a typical English middle-class Christmas, everyone sat around a roaring fire in the lounge enjoying a drink after dinner on Christmas Eve. The room was dominated by a large tastefully decorated Christmas tree, under which a number of presents sat in their brightly coloured wrapping paper. Peter had always got on well with Mathew's sister Judith and the two of them drifted off to the kitchen to refill their glasses, whilst the rest of her family settled down for a game of cards. Judith and Gloria had become good friends over the years and she was keen to find out how Peter had been coping since her death.

"I struggled with it for a long time Judy, but during the last few months it's as though a cloud has been lifted from above my head. Your brother's been a great help, he has the patience of a saint!" Peter told her.

"He told me that you've started doing a bit of work again on defence matters and helped Robert Coleville with his memoirs." Judith said.

"Well, only on one chapter, he wanted some help on the Ambrose affair and I worked on that story all those years ago."

"You've always been modest Peter, you did more than work on it, it was your story! I worked for Coleville for a while you know." Judith said.

"Really, I didn't know that." Peter said, surprised.

"It wasn't long after the Ambrose affair actually, the department was in a right mess and I was seconded from the Home Office to help out with some research he needed doing."

"How did you find him?" Peter asked

"I liked him, he had this reputation for being a bit of a smoothy and a womaniser, but I didn't see that side of him at all at the time. Sure, he was a handsome man, who could be a bit vain, but you know, I found him very professional and actually, very kind. I remember one day, I'd prepared a presentation for him to give to some committee and he asked me to be on hand at the meeting to answer any detailed questions that arose. Anyway, Archie's boarding school rang me on the morning of the meeting and told me he'd been taken ill during the night, food poisoning I think it was. Robert told me I must leave for the school immediately, I reminded him about the presentation and that I needed to be there, but he wouldn't hear of it. In fact, he had access to one of the minister's cars at the time and got the chauffer to drive me straight to the school! Probably broke all the rules, but it was like that in those days."

"I had dinner at his house recently, actually it was at his son's house, he wanted to thank me for helping him with the book, all his family were there. Did you keep in touch with him when you left?" Peter asked.

"No, but I did see him a few years later and I suppose it changed my opinion of him a bit, unfairly probably. I'd left the Civil Service by then and was working in the City in the NatWest Tower, I've always been a keen swimmer as you know and the bank used to have a swimming pool in the basement of the tower, so I'd take a late lunch and go for a swim when the pool was quieter." Judith poured them both another glass of wine. "I used to do lanes in the pool in those days and on that day had the pool to myself, I was just about to get out and take a shower, when in walked Robert with a very attractive blonde woman. They sat on the edge of the pool at one end with their legs dangling over the side into the water. She was quite a bit younger than Robert and at first, I thought it might be a relative, a niece perhaps, but it soon became clear that she wasn't. It was their body language. They weren't snogging or anything like that, but I just knew that they were a couple, they looked so happy together, I always remember that."

"Did he recognise you?" Peter asked

"No, when I first spotted him, whilst I was swimming, he looked at me and I half expected him to wave or something, but then I remembered that I was wearing a swimming cap and goggles and he wouldn't have recognised me. When I got out of the pool I went straight to the changing rooms, it would have seemed wrong to intrude and as I said, they looked so happy together."

After a splendid Christmas Day lunch all of the family, with the exception of Mathew's parents, went for a walk. It was another cold bright sunny day, but by the time they had left the house it was already three o'clock and would be dark in an hour's time. Mathew walked with his older brother John, who had arrived that morning and they spent the whole time deep in conversation. With John living in the highlands of Scotland and Mathew in London, it was a rare chance for the brothers to catch up with each other's news. Peter found himself being quizzed during the walk by Archie and Tom, they both worked in the Civil Service and were keen to speak with such an authority on defence matters. Peter was only too pleased to answer their questions as best he could.

When they all returned to the house, Mathew's parents had poured them all a glass of mulled wine to enjoy with mince pies. Peter thought of his own parents, who had both died within a week of each other when they were in their eighties. Whilst they both came from very different backgrounds to Mathew's parents, he could see many similarities between them. He thought there were generational reasons behind the similarities, common amongst men and women who had lived through the Second World War. Mathew had told Peter that he had noticed it when he used to visit his parents in Birmingham. It was also the first time that Peter had seen Mathew's parents since Gloria had passed away, they loved Gloria's company and he could detect a slight sadness when he spoke with them.

During the drive back to London, the old friends reflected on their break in Surrey and discussed their plans for the next few weeks. Mathew was keen to hear about Peter's date with Isabella and was pleased to hear that they were planning to meet again.

"By the way, without giving any details away, I spoke with my brother about the best way of finding out about births back in the Seventies," Mathew said, "we discussed the obvious methods, official registrations, announcements in local and national papers and so on. Anyway, he gave me the phone number of a contact in the NHS in London who might be able to help if we get stuck. He didn't say, but I suspect it's a contact from his days in the Met. John was very senior by the time he retired you know."

"Chief Inspector, I remember you telling me a few years ago when he took his pension." added Peter.

"I'll give you a ring with any news as soon as I've found out anything Peter."

CHAPTER ELEVEN

JULIA

Julia returned from the gym, it had been closed over Christmas and she had felt sluggish without her daily workout and swim. She had treated herself to a takeaway cappuccino and croissant, which she put on the table whilst she switched on her mobile phone. There was a text message from Robert, confirming that he would be coming around at lunchtime and an email from Erik in New York, telling her that the bank had confirmed that they wanted him to stay in the States for at least the next two months.

Perhaps it was the start of a new year, but Julia felt reflective and thought back to her arrival in London from Stockholm in 1972, aged eighteen. Her childhood in Sweden had been problematic and at times, traumatic. She was abandoned as a baby by her mother, who suffered from mental illness and alcoholism. She had no idea who her father was. Having spent periods of time in children's homes and with foster parents, she was eventually adopted by a kind couple, when she was twelve. At sixteen, her adoptive mother died of a brain hemorrhage and although her adoptive father did his best to look after her, like most teenagers she was going through a difficult period herself and their relationship became fractured. On her eighteenth birthday, Julia left Sweden for England, she was blonde, Swedish and extremely good looking and had little problem finding work as an au pair in nineteen-seventies London. On the day she left Stockholm her adoptive father gave her the equivalent of five hundred pounds in Swedish Krona, a large sum of money at the time. Within three months of arriving in London, Julia found herself pregnant, following a one night stand and she soon discovered that pregnant au pairs were not so welcome, even in liberal-minded Hampstead. She became homeless and without work. She used some of the money her father had given her to put down as a deposit on a rented, one bedroom flat in Hampstead and found work waitressing at a greasy spoon café in Swiss Cottage. This would do until the baby arrived, she decided.

Whilst Julia's pregnancy was uneventful, the birth was anything but. Apart from mild jaundice, the baby was healthy. Julia, on the other hand, suffered life threatening complications during the birth and spent more than a fortnight in the maternity hospital, before being discharged with her child. She didn't see her baby boy for more than a week after giving birth. The doctors had difficulty treating her at times, partly because they had no medical records for her and because she had been adopted, no hereditary information was available regarding her health. Julia had not given any information regarding next of kin to the hospital when she was admitted and was completely alone. However, she was young and strong and eventually made a full recovery.

When she returned home to her flat in Hampstead with her baby, whom she had called Erik after her adoptive father, she soon realised that, somehow, she would have to find some kind of work. The money her father had given her would not last forever. Her luck changed when the district nurse, who visited her regularly at home following her discharge from hospital, told her that the local library was looking for staff to work on a part-time basis. Importantly for Julia, the local Council had recently opened a crèche, next door to the library, to help mothers get back to work. It was an opportunity she couldn't miss and she immediately walked around to the library to enquire about the vacancies, leaving Erik with the district nurse for an hour! Julia already spoke good English before she arrived in London and by the time she applied for the job in the library her English was virtually perfect. Following an interview a few days later, she was offered the job on a three month trial basis. Julia enjoyed working at the library and mothering Erik. He was good baby, he slept well and was happy when she left him at the crèche whilst she was working. For the first time in her life, she felt in control of events and vowed that for Erik's and her own sake, she would remain in control of her life for as long as she lived.

Julia's probation period at the library passed quickly and successfully. The library had started to open on Saturday mornings and the head librarian had asked Julia if she would like to work some extra hours. The crèche was open on Saturday mornings and Julia jumped at the chance of earning some extra money. It was on one of those Saturday mornings in early July that she met Robert for the first time. She had noticed the tall, handsome man looking through the local history and political sections. When he had chosen the books he wanted to lend, he took them to the counter where Julia was working, handed her his library ticket and also asked if she would reserve another book for him and told her he would pick it up the next time he visited the library. A similar pattern occurred over the next few weeks and Julia couldn't help feeling attracted to the handsome man, even though she thought he must have been at least ten years older than her. On most days, she took her break at eleven o'clock and would pop into the café around the corner from the library for a cup of tea and a couple of slices of toast. It was on a very wet morning, when she was enjoying her break that the handsome man came into the café, he seemed surprised to see Julia, smiled and asked whether he could join her. The café was crowded with customers who had decided to shelter from the downpour and there were no free tables, so Julia smiled and nodded. He left his dripping wet umbrella next to the table by the steamed up window, where Julia was sat and before going to the counter to place his order, he asked whether she would like another cup of tea. Robert returned to the table and introduced himself. The young waitress arrived with more tea for Julia and a large plate of toast and jam. Their relationship, which would last for more than forty years started that wet morning over tea and toast in the small café near the library.

Julia sat in the kitchen of her modern apartment in Bayswater, enjoying her cappuccino and croissant and reflected on her unusual relationship with Robert. She remembered that, from the outset, he had told her the truth about his life. He was a Member of Parliament, married to Margaret with a young child and lived, like her at the time, in Hampstead. Despite the enormous risks he was taking with his career and more importantly, his marriage, he had chosen to share part of his life with her. It was true that the media attention on Members of Parliament in the nineteen-seventies was less intrusive than it would become in later years, but there were still big risks involved, for both of them, in those early days of their relationship. Julia accepted that their relationship was unusual, but in forty years he had asked for nothing more from her than love and affection and she had asked for nothing more than that from him. She still wondered occasionally whether, if she had experienced a more loving and caring upbringing, her attitude towards Robert and men generally would have been different. Would she have accepted their relationship, when they first met, if she didn't have a young child to look after? Looking back, she remembered that sometimes they would go weeks or, even months without seeing each other. As an MP, Robert was extremely busy working and he also had a wife and young child at home and Julia had little time to herself in those early days, she was also working and looking after Erik on her own. On reflection, she was surprised that they managed to see each other at all in those early days. Then there was the subterfuge. At times, she had felt terribly sad and anxious at the prospect of their relationship being discovered, but interestingly, she found that, as time passed, she became used to the situation. Robert told her recently that he had experienced the same emotions. Much later on in their relationship technology, such as mobile phones, texting and emails, made life much easier. For the first twenty years or so they relied on hurried landline telephone calls to speak with each other and make any arrangements to meet and Julia smiled when she remembered that they actually used to write letters to each other from time to time, even though they were living in the same city and early on in the relationship, in the same district of London! She still had a large bundle of letters that Robert had sent her. Some of the happiest times were when Erik was young and she would take him with her for weekends at the seaside in Sussex, near to Robert's constituency. He would spend most weekends in his parliamentary constituency, usually on his own, at the family cottage. It gave them the opportunity to be together, Erik was too young to really understand their relationship.

There were darker times though, when she tried to better understand Robert's relationship with his wife, Margaret. He had told her, from the beginning of their relationship, that he would never leave his wife, which puzzled her. Thinking about it logically, how could he be so sure that he would never leave her or, that she wouldn't leave him for that matter? She used to think that there was something that kept their marriage intact that she had missed, it was almost as though the two of them had agreed some kind of pact that couldn't be broken. Eventually, she decided, much in the same way that she had vowed to herself that she would always be in control of her life, she simply wouldn't think about Robert's relationship with his wife. After all, he wasn't the kind of man who was constantly complaining that his wife didn't understand him. In fact, he only ever mentioned Margaret if it affected their own relationship, perhaps she would be going without him to the farmhouse in Italy for a few weeks, which she did more often as the years passed.

Certainly, over the years, Robert had been generous as far as Erik was concerned. By the time Erik was at school age, they had decided that it would be better if he wasn't present whenever they met. However, that didn't prevent Robert helping pay for the young boy's school fees and consequently, he had a first class education. When Erik completed his university education, Julia was fairly sure that Robert had worked behind the scenes and opened a few doors for him, helping him to get the job at the bank, although Robert would never own up to this. When Erik had gone to boarding school, Robert told her about job opportunities at the House of Commons and she found well paid work there and similarly, a few years later he helped her to get a job at a bank in The City. Julia remembered drawing the line at accepting money from Robert. When he encouraged her to buy the apartment in Bayswater, she accepted the deposit for the flat that he offered purely on a loan basis, albeit interest free! By the start of the new millennium, she had repaid his loan in full. One of her most satisfying achievements was successfully studying to become an accountant during the nineteen-nineties. It took her the best part of five years to qualify and now she had her own company, which she ran from the apartment in Bayswater, providing accountancy services to a dozen or so small companies.

Julia finished her coffee and whilst she did the washing up, thought back to the day when, as a young eighteen year old foreigner living in London, she was offered the job at the library and made the vow to remain in control of her life for the rest of her days. Now, approaching sixty, she was delighted that she still felt in control.

CHAPTER TWELVE

THE ATTIC

Isabella had cooked pollo al ajillo, garlic chicken, using her grandmother's recipe, Peter had brought the wine, a very good Rioja, which had complemented the food. They had finished the desert of fresh fruit and were enjoying coffee in the lounge of Isabella's Hampstead home. Whilst she was a neighbour of the Colevilles, her house was more modest, but beautifully furnished in a modern style. The couple had carried on where they left off when they had met just before Christmas, Peter felt totally relaxed in Isabella's company and he had a strong feeling that she felt the same about him. Their relationship felt very natural to Peter.

Sitting next to each other on the sofa, Isabella asked Peter about his career.

"I was a defence correspondent first and foremost I suppose," Peter explained, "that paid the bills, but my real passion has always been investigative journalism and over the years, I managed to work on some great stories with a good team and managed to combine the work with the 'day job' on defence. When I arrived in Fleet Street in the nineteen seventies, working for a newspaper was very different to what it is today, less professional, but more exciting I suppose you could say. I guess I was lucky to catch the back end of all that, before the modernisation took over and they all left Fleet Street."

Isabella could tell that Peter didn't really like speaking about himself too much and smiled.

"You're being very modest Peter, I googled you and saw that you won several awards for journalism!" Isabella laughed.

"Well, as I said, I had a good team around me, anyway enough about me, tell me how you met the Colevilles?" Peter asked hoping to change the subject.

"I moved in five years ago Peter and almost immediately, I was invited by another neighbour to a coffee morning where I met Margaret. She had recently retired and had time on her hands, she told me she spent more and more time over in Italy staying in their farmhouse. Anyway, they would entertain at their house, this is before they sold it to Simon and Pat and they would invite me occasionally. To be honest, I think they thought it would be a good idea to invite a divorcee along whenever single men were also invited!" Isabella laughed.

"Well, I'm just sorry it took me so long to turn up!" Peter joked

"Yes, me too, where have you been all this time!" Isabella smiled and Peter reached over and held her hand. "Anyway, I soon got to know the family, Robert is a real sweetie and I've struck up a good friendship with Pat since she moved in with Simon. I like Margaret, but to be honest, how do you say in English, she is hard work?"

Peter nodded and smiled knowingly.

"I get this odd feeling that she is always preoccupied about something, kind of distant. I spoke with Pat about it one day and she just laughed and said that's just Margaret's way. Peter, I'm sorry, listen to me gossiping about my neighbours, you must think I'm terrible!"

"On the contrary, I think you are lovely Isabella," Peter said and leant over and kissed her gently on the cheek, "but, I have outstayed my welcome and must call a cab."

"Thank you Peter," and Isabella returned the kiss, "I am really touched, promise me that we will meet again soon?"

"I promise, I would really like that Isabella." Peter replied.

When Peter got back home to Marylebone he checked his mobile phone for any messages and saw a text from Mathew, telling him that he had some news about January 1973 and suggested a meeting at *The Elephant and Castle* tomorrow lunchtime.

Unusually, Peter arrived at *The Elephant and Castle* before Mathew and had a pint of bitter waiting for him on their table when he arrived. Mathew looked at his watch as he came into the pub.

"Have I forgotten that the clocks have gone forward old boy?" he joked as he took his seat opposite Peter.

Peter laughed and passed Mathew the menu for the day. Mathew ordered fish and chips and Peter, again unusually for him, ordered a ham salad and before Mathew asked, Peter explained.

"Isabella cooked a delicious garlic chicken last night and it was rather filling."

Mathew could tell his old friend had a spring in his step and he was pleased for him. As soon as they had finished their meals, they got down to business.

"So, what have you got?" Peter asked.

"Well, it's very interesting, I ended up getting the information from a number of sources. Firstly, Margaret Coleville definitely gave birth in Hampstead on the 15th of January 1973. An announcement was placed in the Daily Telegraph on Friday the 19th, which read, *'On 15th January 1973, in Hampstead, to Margaret and Robert Coleville a first son, Simon Roland.'* I felt it was worth confirming that Simon was definitely born on the 15th before continuing with the searches." Mathew said.

"Of course, good idea Matt." Peter replied, remembering how thorough Mathew was and how it was often important

86

to get the smallest details correct. For some reason, he suddenly thought of Sidney Newman and smiled!

"The 15th of January 1973 was a Monday and I discovered four other births, all between the 12th and 18th of January, at the maternity hospital where Margaret gave birth. The good news is that two of those four births were girls, so presumably we can discount those?" Mathew asked. Peter nodded and Mathew continued. "So, two other mothers gave birth to boys, both of them, as it turns out, on the 15th of January. Stella Farell, aged twenty-eight, gave birth to a boy they called Gregory. Stella and her husband Wesley announced it in the Ham & High local newspaper. The other birth was to a mother called Julia Norberg, aged eighteen, but there were no announcements that I could find and therefore, no record of the baby's name."

"You mentioned that you got the information from a number of sources Matt, did that include the contact your brother gave you?" Peter asked.

"I won't go into details, but yes it did and I would class it as a highly reliable source." Mathew confirmed.

"Great work Matt, thank you, so I guess the next step is to try and trace the two mothers, Farell and Norberg. Stella Farell would now be nearly seventy and Norberg, nearly sixty, so there is a good chance that they are both still alive and may and I stress may, each have a son alive who was born on the 15th of January 1973." Peter took a sip of beer and looked deep in thought.

"And if we do trace them and they both have a son alive aged about forty?" Mathew asked raising his eyebrows.

"I think we need to make an assumption for the time being Matt, it's quite a big one, but we should assume that the baby that Margaret gave birth to lived. Therefore, if Margaret deliberately took home either Farell's or Norberg's child, did one of them inadvertently take home Margaret's baby. We know that Farell definitely took home 'a' baby, because they called him Gregory and announced the birth in the local paper. At this stage, we don't know whether Norberg took home a baby from the hospital."

"Why ever would Margaret deliberately take home another mother's child and how on earth could she have got away with it in the maternity hospital?" Mathew wondered aloud.

"The motive is unclear at present, but getting away with it may not have been so difficult, after all, who would ever suspect a Member of Parliament's wife of doing something like that?"

"How do you want to take this forward then Peter?" Mathew asked.

"Leave it with me for a few days Matt, I've met some of the people involved in this mystery, Robert, Margaret and Simon Coleville and want to give it a bit more thought, you could get us both another pint though, that would be helpful!" Peter smiled.

Patricia Coleville climbed the steps up to the attic. It was a large space and had been boarded out some years ago, so it was easy to move around. She had left the door to the attic open so that she could hear Emily, who was asleep in the nursery, if she woke up. Simon had gone into the office and had told her that he would not be home until early evening. Patricia had decided to spend an hour or so sorting through one or two of the packing crates, that they still hadn't managed to unpack since they moved into their Hampstead home. There were still various item of furniture that belonged to Robert and Margaret stored in the attic, because there was no room in their new Chelsea home for them. Presumably, at some point, they would sell them, Patricia thought to herself. She walked across to one of the corners of the attic to get a better look at two Victorian button back armchairs. She had been wondering for a little while whether they should offer her in-laws something for them and put them in one of the spare bedrooms. They had been covered with clear plastic sheeting to protect them, but on closer inspection, she noticed that some of the sheeting had come loose and fallen behind one of the armchairs. She went behind the armchair to retrieve the sheeting, where she noticed a large wooden trunk that she hadn't seen before. Something else that Robert and Margaret had left behind she thought! She bent down and opened the trunk and sure enough it was full of bedding and what looked like curtain material. They were all beautiful quality, mostly from *Liberty*, she noticed. As she was sorting through them she came across two buff coloured concertina files. She yanked them out of the trunk and in doing so, the contents of one of the files spilt over the boarded attic floor, papers going everywhere. As she thought, on closer inspection, they were Robert's and labelled 'Constituency Files 1974-78 and 1979-81. Exasperated, Particia got down on her hands and knees and started scooping up the papers and carefully placing them back in the files, although she paid little attention to which sections, which were in alphabetic order, to which she returned them. Suddenly, her eye caught an old slightly faded yellow *Kodak* photo wallet amongst the papers and out of curiosity, she opened it and looked inside. It contained half a dozen photographs, the first of which contained a picture of a small child playing on a beach, he looked about three or four years old and was building a sandcastle. Walking towards the young boy from the shore was a beautiful young blonde woman carrying a bucket, full to the brim with sea water. She was smiling and looking straight ahead of her, not at the child but presumably at the photographer Patricia thought. She turned the photo over and handwritten on the back in black ink it said 'Camber Sands 1977'. She thumbed through the other photographs and there were three more of the blonde woman and child on the beach, all marked on the back 'Camber Sands 1977'. The other two photographs were both of the same boy, by the look of things, but he was noticeably older, perhaps seven or eight and was dressed in, what looked like, a brand new school uniform. Grey shorts and socks, navy blue blazer, white shirt with a blue and gold striped tie. On the back of the two photos it simply said '1981'. Patricia looked through the photographs again, the young blonde woman looked as though she was in her early twenties and although she couldn't be sure, she didn't think she looked English. Possibly Dutch or German or, even Scandinavian, Patricia thought. There was something else about the woman and the child that slightly unnerved her, she felt as though she recognised both of them. Patricia then did something that, when she thought about it later, totally surprised her. She went back downstairs, checked that Emily was still asleep and found her mobile phone, which she had left on the table on the landing. She quickly went back up to the attic and laid the six photographs out in a line on the boarded attic floor. She found herself shaking slightly and had to compose herself for a moment, before taking a photo of each picture with her mobile phone. She then put the photographs back in the faded *Kodak* photo wallet, which she placed in one of the concertina files. Finally, she put the two concertina files back in the wooden trunk underneath the bedding and curtain material and closed the trunk.

Following the lunch with Mathew, Peter switched on his laptop in the study of his home in Marylebone. He started undertaking a series of searches using the *Google* search engine and was surprised at how quickly he got results, although he acknowledged that there was an element of luck involved in the process. He started by typing in *Stella Farell* and was provided with an array of *Facebook*, and *Linkedin* profiles and a *New York Times* report on a housewife of that name, who had given birth to quadruplets. None of these results were of any use. Peter tried a few more searches which also were of little help, before he

90

refined the search typing in *Stella, Wesley, Gregory Farell, London* in the search bar. The first result he saw was a report from a North London newspaper on a service at a local Evangelical church. Peter read that Wesley and Stella Farell and their son Gregory, along with three grandchildren, had helped raise £15,450 towards the retiling of the church roof. There was even a photograph of the Farells with the Pastor outside the church and as Peter had expected after reading the article, the Farell's were of Afro-Caribbean descent. Both Wesley and Stella had emigrated from Trinidad to the United Kingdom in 1967. Stella Farell had definitely not taken Margaret Coleville's baby home from the maternity hospital, she took home her own son, Gregory.

The search for Julia Norberg wasn't quite as easy. There was at least twenty entries on *Facebook* and *Linkedin,* as well as endless pages of Scandinavian search results. Peter refined the search and typed in *Julia Norberg London.* There were several entries and Peter started trawling through each one, until he opened a *Companies House* entry for 'Julia Norberg Accountancy Limited'. It gave details of the incorporated company, which had one shareholder, confirmation that the accounts for the previous year had been made up and importantly, that it had one Director, an accountant, Julia Norberg born 1954. To Peter's surprise it even listed a correspondence address for the company in Bayswater. Peter printed the page containing the details, switched off the laptop and poured himself a large scotch.

CHAPTER THIRTEEN

THE COMPANY ACCOUNTS

Robert Coleville set the burglar alarm and double locked the front door of the house in Chelsea. Margaret was still at the farmhouse in Italy and he had been invited to Sunday lunch in Hampstead by Simon and Patricia. He decided to take the tube from Sloane Square, changing at Embankment. He had turned seventy the previous year and now that his memoirs had been dispatched to the publisher he found, for the first time in his life, that he had time on his hands. Consequently, he had been reflecting on some of the more unusual aspects of his life, very little of which had been included in his memoirs.

Robert's grandparents had fled from Odessa, now part of the Ukraine, in the late nineteenth century and eventually settled in East London. His grandfather was a tailor and setup a business shortly after arriving in London and passed the business on to Robert's father just after the end of the First World War. The family business prospered and at one point it employed as many as seventy workers in Spitalfields, in what was then known as the rag trade. Robert's parents lived in Spitalfields throughout this period. They eventually sold the business during the nineteen-fifties for a huge profit and with some of the proceeds, bought the beautiful house in Hampstead, which in turn was passed on to Robert, their only child, when he graduated from Cambridge University in 1965, he was just twenty-two years old. His parents moved to a smaller house in Golders Green, where they lived out their last few years together amongst the Jewish community. Whilst Robert felt

Jewish, he had never practiced his religion. His parents had liberal views concerning religion and in any case, were too busy building up the family business and concentrating on giving Robert a good education to be concerned over their son's lack of interest in religion. Robert did well at school and was a popular student amongst his classmates. He won a place at Cambridge University and studied history, where he graduated with an upper second honours degree. Whilst at Cambridge, he had become interested in politics and joined the Conservative Party and it was at a Conservative Association meeting that he met Margaret. She was a year younger than Robert, intelligent and extremely attractive. They were often described in University magazines as the best looking couple at Cambridge during the early nineteen-sixties. Margaret's family had a strong military background and whist she wasn't interested in politics, joining the Conservative Party and attending Conservative Association meetings was the 'done thing' for a girl from her background. Years later, she jokingly told Robert that the reason she had agreed to go out with him was because he was the least boring person at one of the association meetings she had attended! Margaret studied chemistry at Cambridge and graduated with a first-class honours degree.

By the time they married in 1968, both of Robert's parents had passed away. Robert was working full time for the Conservative Party at their headquarters in Smith Square, Westminster and would have to wait another two years before being elected as a Member of Parliament, for a constituency in Sussex, in 1970. At twenty-seven, he was one of the youngest ever Conservative MPs. Within twelve months of becoming an MP he was working as a junior minister at the Ministry of Defence and was being tipped to have a great future ahead of him. One of the Sunday newspapers even suggested that he was future Prime Minister material, a great intellect, young, wealthy, good looking with a beautiful wife. However, behind this veneer of success, pressure was beginning to build up and tragedy was to follow. Robert and Margaret had been trying for a baby since they married and in early 1970, Margaret became pregnant but suffered a miscarriage after seven weeks. Both of them struggled to understand why this had happened, they had been told by the specialist in Harley Street that there were no underlying problems. In the immediate aftermath, Margaret suffered from a brief period of depression. Worse was to follow. Later that year, Margaret fell pregnant again and all went well until six months into the pregnancy when Margaret was rushed to hospital, where the baby was stillborn. Margaret fell into deep depression and experienced terrible feelings of guilt. She blamed herself for being unable to give birth to a healthy baby. Robert was loving and supportive during this period, but was unable to reassure his wife that it was not her fault. Eventually, he threw himself further into his work in Parliament to take his mind off these terrible events. Mrs. Jeffreys, the housekeeper, who had been with them since they married in 1968 and previously had worked for Margaret's parents, cared for her at home during this difficult time. Margaret fell pregnant for the third and last time twelve months later and following a trouble-free but anxious pregnancy, gave birth to a baby boy on the 15th of January 1973. It should have been the happiest time of Robert's life, but within forty-eight hours of the birth it had turned into a nightmare, that would live with them both for the next forty years.

Peter and Mathew took their drinks from the bar and settled into their favourite seats in *The Elephant and Castle*. Peter passed Mathew a printout of a draft email he had prepared earlier that morning, which he was planning to send to Julia Norberg Accountancy Limited. His plan was to engineer a face-to-face meeting with Julia Norberg and to achieve this, he would pose as a potential client who wanted his annual accounts prepared and required a quote. Mathew reviewed the draft text and suggested one or two changes.

"Perhaps you should mention that your existing accountant is moving abroad old boy, you've already said in the draft that you found her business through a search on *Google* and this would explain why you were looking for an accountant in the first place, adds to the authenticity. Oh and I wouldn't mention how much your accountant charged you last year, might put her off seeing you if it falls short of her usual rates!"

"Good suggestions Matt." Peter replied, whilst scribbling on the draft that Mathew had passed back to him.

"And if you do get to meet Julia Norberg, what then?" Mathew asked, intrigued.

"Oh, I just want to get a good look at her to start with, I have a feeling that will tell us a lot, shall I order the food, they've got bangers and mash on?" Peter smiled.

Patricia had prepared roast lamb for lunch, Robert's favourite. She was a good cook and the three of them enjoyed the Sunday roast, whilst Emily was asleep upstairs in the nursery. They ate in the kitchen and Simon and Robert finished a bottle of red wine between them during the meal. Robert insisted on helping Patricia with the washing up after lunch, whilst Simon went upstairs to look after Emily. Robert was very fond of Patricia and was delighted when Simon met her. She was a gentle person and he recognised the calming influence she had on the family. He loved Simon and throughout his childhood, he had been determined to do everything possible for him and treat him like any other father would treat their son. Sometimes he would over compensate, probably through guilt he often thought, but what father didn't spoil their son occasionally? As Simon grew up, Robert was extremely happy that they had actually become very good friends. Sometimes he questioned whether this was normal in a father/son relationship and he would often watch how other fathers behaved with their grown up sons to reassure himself that nothing out of the ordinary was occurring. Afterwards, he would chide himself for such ridiculous behaviour. Some of his happiest moments over the past few years had been sharing a pint of beer with Simon at their local pub in Hampstead. He felt totally at ease in Simon's company and he was sure that this feeling was reciprocated. He accepted that Margaret's relationship with Simon was always going to be more complex than his own relationship with him. She had always been a good mother, loving and kind towards him and if, at times, she could appear cool and slightly distant in his company, Robert wondered whether that was just her nature and she would have behaved the same if Simon had been her own son? What had surprised and delighted Robert was Margaret's sheer joy when Emily arrived. He had never seen such a doting grandmother, it was as though the arrival of a new generation in the family had almost legitimised her relationship with Simon and perhaps, in Margaret's mind, Emily really was her granddaughter.

"Let me wash and you dry Pat." Robert offered, he felt pleasantly relaxed after drinking the wine. Patricia, passed Robert an apron with a smile and picked up a tea towel.

"Oh, by the way Robert, I was up in the attic earlier in the week, believe it or not we're still unpacking," Patricia explained, "you know you've still got a lot of furniture up there, I was looking at that pair of Victorian button-back armchairs, they're lovely Robert and would look great in Chelsea you know."

"I'm sorry Pat, as soon as Margaret is back from Italy I'll speak with her and decide what to do with them and the other furniture up there, you know if there's anything you and Simon fancy, you only have to ask."

"Thank you Robert, there's no rush, anyway whilst I was up there I came across a large trunk which you must have forgotten to take with you, it's mostly full of bedding and curtain materials, but there was some of your files in there as well." Patricia sensed a slight tension in the air as she spoke.

"I'll pop up there and have a quick look when we've finished the washing up Pat," Robert replied, "I can make a mental note of all the furniture whilst I'm up there and then talk to Margaret about what we're going to do with it."

As soon as Robert opened the trunk, lifted out the materials and saw the two concertina files, the alarm bells started ringing in his head. He lifted both of the files out of the trunk and started thumbing through each section alphabetically. As soon as he saw the faded *Kodak* photograph wallet he cursed himself for his forgetfulness. He didn't need to look inside the wallet, he knew exactly what they contained. He slipped it into the inside pocket of his jacket and put the concertina files back in the trunk. On returning downstairs, Patricia and Simon were enjoying a coffee. Emily was sat smiling in the buggy next to them.

"Thanks for reminding me about the trunk up there Pat, old constituency papers, they need shredding really, I'll bring the car over next time and take them and some of the other stuff up there back to Chelsea." Robert said.

"There's no urgency dad, coffee?" asked Simon

"No, I really must be getting back, but thanks all the same, I've had a lovely time thanks to you two, or three I should say!" Robert said smiling at Emily.

The next morning after Simon had left for the office, Patricia climbed the stairs to the attic, went over to where the Victorian armchairs were sat, opened the old trunk and took out the two concertina files and started looking through them. Sure enough, the *Kodak* photograph wallet was missing.

97

The email from Julia Norberg Accountancy Limited was sat in Peter's inbox on his laptop when he logged on, the morning after his lunchtime meeting with Mathew. He was slightly surprised to see it sitting there under the subject heading 'The Company Accounts'. Peter opened the email and read that Julia Norberg thanked him for his enquiry and said she would be delighted to provide him with a quote for preparing his annual company accounts. She suggested that they should meet and he should bring some high level details about his company, e.g. the type of company, approximate annual income and overheads and if he felt comfortable, perhaps a recent balance sheet. There would be no obligation on him she stressed and providing they both intended to proceed, she would submit a written quote, by email or by post, within five working days. She suggested a meeting in the ground floor reception area at the *Hilton London Paddington Hotel* on Praed Street and included three potential dates, with times, when she would be available to meet. The email concluded with some legal information and was closed, 'Best Regards Julia Norberg (ICAEW)'.

Peter re-read the email and thought that she probably runs her business from the company's address in Bayswater, which was also most likely her home.

Robert had returned home following Sunday lunch with Simon and Patricia feeling annoyed with himself. Why on earth hadn't he remembered that he had hidden the photographs in his constituency files all those years ago? He had spent the best part of forty years taking meticulous care over such matters and prided himself at how careful he had been and how successful he had been in covering his tracks. He put it down to old age, after all he was in his seventies now. He went into the kitchen feeling thoroughly miserable and poured himself a large scotch. Anyway, he thought in an attempt to cheer himself up, perhaps Pat didn't even see the photographs and even if she had, so what, he wasn't in any of them. On the other hand, if she hadn't seen them, would she have even taken the trouble to mention the trunk and the concertina files? The house in Hampstead was cluttered with stuff that they had left behind when they move to Chelsea and Pat had never mentioned a word about any of it until now.

Robert finished his scotch and feeling slightly more cheerful looked through the photographs. He remembered taking the pictures on Camber Sands. It was a part of East Sussex that he had visited with Julia many times over the past forty years, a special place. In the early days they would take Erik with them and enjoy a picnic on the beach. Julia looked beautiful in the picture and he remembered, around this time, encouraging her to embark on a modelling career, he knew a few people in the fashion world and he could help, but she would just laugh at him and tell him to stop being so ridiculous. In later years, when Erik had gone to boarding school or, even later when he had grown up and left home they would go alone and walk arm in arm along the beach. The photographs on the beach were taken in 1977, when Erik was four. Christ! He looked so much like Margaret back then, he thought to himself.

He looked at the other photos of Erik taken in 1981, when he was eight, it was his first day at boarding school and Robert noticed, not for the first time, that Erik had begun to look like him. Julia had taken the photographs outside the school gates, using his camera he remembered. He also remembered insisting that she used his camera to take the pictures, so that he would have an excuse to get them developed and keep copies for himself. He had told Julia that his camera was very expensive, which it was, and took a better photograph than her camera. She had replied, in typical Julia style, that he had never seen a photograph taken with her camera, so how did he know that his camera was better? Just trust me, he had told her and they both laughed. Robert felt himself drifting off to sleep and thought to himself that Julia had always trusted him and for some reason, that he had never fully understood, he had always trusted her.

From the moment Peter set eyes on Julia Norberg he knew that she was the birth mother of Simon Coleville. It was her eyes. Julia, like Simon, had unusual grey/blue coloured eyes. When she spoke, her English was perfect with no discernible foreign accent and it was impossible to tell that she wasn't English. However, her looks and surname clearly indicated that she had Scandinavian blood, probably Swedish Peter thought.

They were sat together in the café on the ground floor of the *Hilton London, Paddington Hotel*. Julia was extremely professional and businesslike and asked Peter a series of questions about his company, ticking off each question and making notes on a small notepad as he answered.

"Do you have many clients?" Peter asked in an attempt to force her to stop ticking boxes.

Julia smiled, "I have a dozen or so smallish clients and I prepare their accounts from my office at home in Bayswater." she replied, before taking a sip of her coffee that the waiter had just brought.

She was a very attractive woman Peter thought and could easily be in her mid-forties, rather than approaching sixty. He wondered how she had ended up in London in 1973, aged eighteen, giving birth to a baby boy. It hardly seemed to fit in with the confident, sophisticated business woman sat in front of him. When she had completed her 'questionnaire' she asked Peter about his work and he saw no reason why he shouldn't give her a potted history of his career in journalism, she would probably '*google*' him later anyway, if she hadn't already done so he reckoned. She made no notes whilst he talked, but he noticed that she was listening carefully and probably weighing up whether he was the kind of client she would want to do business with. When he had finished, she complimented him on being such a successful journalist, and Peter smiled, thinking that she almost certainly had '*googled*' him earlier! He asked whether she would like another coffee, but it was clear from her body language that the meeting was coming to a close. Julia thanked him for the copy of the balance sheet from an earlier year that he was leaving with her to help with the preparation of the quote and she told him that she would email him within five working days, if that was alright with him. Peter smiled and thanked her, all the time thinking about Taraneh Saderzadeh and the strange story she had told him more than forty years ago.

Robert was sat in Julia's kitchen drinking a cup of tea, whilst she was busy baking a cake.

"I'm free to come over tomorrow if you like Julia, Margaret's still in Italy, we could plan that trip down to Sussex we've been thinking about. We haven't been down there for ages and you know how much we enjoy ourselves there." Sussex had been on Robert's mind since he had looked through the photographs that he recovered from the attic.

"Could we plan that later in the week love, I met a new potential client yesterday and I would like to prepare the quote for him tomorrow, you don't mind do you?" Julia asked.

Robert didn't answer, his attention had been caught by the papers sat next to him on the kitchen table, particularly what looked like a balance sheet, on which Julia had scribbled in pencil, 'Peter Wilson, journalist, quote by Monday.'

"You're not listening to me are you Robert." Julia said without turning around from the kitchen worktop, where she was preparing the lemon drizzle cake for the oven.

"Sorry Julia, I was miles away, yes that'll be fine we can plan it another day," Robert murmured feeling unsettled, "who is the new client?"

"Oh, a journalist guy, Peter Wilson, used to be fairly well known I think, worked for a few of the broadsheets back in the day, retired now, just does a bit of freelance work for his own company, do you know him?" Julia asked.

"I've heard of him....... when's that cake going to be ready then?" Robert asked, struggling to regain his composure.

When Robert returned home to Chelsea he went into the kitchen and made himself a mug of strong black coffee. He'd felt quite unsettled since discovering that Julia had met Peter Wilson. Perhaps it was a coincidence, he thought to himself. It was the second unsettling incident in a matter of days, firstly, there was Pat stumbling upon the trunk in the attic containing the photographs of Julia and Erik and now this. Were the two incidents connected, he wondered. Peter Wilson had certainly met Pat at the dinner party in Hampstead. He tried to make sense of it all but felt too tired. It wouldn't be the end of the world if either Peter or Pat or, both for that matter discovered that he'd had an affair during his life, most people who knew him would probably be surprised if he hadn't had one! But, what if either of them had discovered something much more serious, it just didn't bear thinking about!

CHAPTER FOURTEEN

TWO SONS

Simon Coleville carried Emily up to the nursery, she had been fed earlier and was already dropping off to sleep as he climbed the stairs with her. He settled Emily in her cot and sat in the armchair next to her. It was the same nursery that he had slept in as a child forty years earlier. Emily started drifting off to sleep and Simon tried to remember his earliest memories, but it was quite difficult. Before he started school, aged five, he had mainly been cared for by Mrs. Jeffreys, the housekeeper. His parents had very busy lives, Mrs. Jeffreys would tell him as he got older. Apparently, there were one or two nannies employed to look after him, he'd seen the photograph on the credenza in the dining room of one of them holding him, but he was much too young to remember either of them. His relationship with his father had always been good he thought. Although, whilst he was growing up Robert was extremely busy as a Member of Parliament, he would always find time for him when it was needed. What he remembered most about his relationship with his father when he was young, was that it was fun. Sometimes they would go days without seeing each other, then suddenly, out of the blue, a day out for the two of them to watch the cricket at Lords had been arranged or, a trip to the British Museum or London Zoo. The days out were always a surprise and happy occasions and would almost always end up with the two of them having a burger or a pizza on the way home. On Christmas morning he would wake up to find his presents in a pillow case at the bottom of his bed and a red stocking filled with chocolates and his favourite sweets. He never once saw his father sneaking into his room and placing them carefully on the blanket box at the bottom of the bed and when he asked him how he did it without waking him up, his father would swear it was Father Christmas who had done it and not him. Simon smiled to himself as he remembered those magical times.

His relationship with his mother was altogether more complex. He knew that she loved him and she was always kind and loving towards him, but he did feel that she was distant sometimes, almost in a world of her own. Simon remembered clearly as he was growing up, he must have been seven or eight, his father telling him that his mother was poorly and the illness she suffered from was called depression. His father reassured him, lovingly, that it was nothing for him to worry about and that his mother would get better. Sometimes, he wouldn't see her for several days because she was too poorly to get out of bed and Mrs. Jeffreys would look after him on a day-to-day basis. Then, as if nothing had happened, his mother would suddenly reappear and everything would be back to normal. As he got older he noticed that his mother's bouts of depression occurred less frequently and she seemed more relaxed around the house. One incident that always stuck in his mind concerned his blonde hair. Whenever friends or family came to visit he was always told what beautiful blonde hair he had and as he grew up it puzzled him. Why haven't my mother and father got blonde hair he thought, they both have very dark hair, so one day he asked his mother. Simon remembered her looking at him for several moments, as though she was thinking about the question very carefully, before telling him that he probably inherited it from his grandfather. It only confused him further, because he'd seen a photograph of grandpa Pennington when he must have been in his forties and he had very dark hair too!

He had noticed that his relationship with his mother seemed to improve when he met Patricia, the two of them get along so well he thought and the trips to the farmhouse in Italy are always something they all to look forward to. The most remarkable change he had seen in his mother happened when Emily was born. He had never, in all his life, seen his mother so happy or relaxed as when she is in Emily's company and he felt pleased that it has brought the family closer together.

Simon remembered being packed off to boarding school when he was eight and his mother's surprise when he didn't cry when they left him at the school in Surrey. He was moved to a minor public school when he was eleven, where he would stay until his seventeenth birthday. He loved boarding school, there was so much to do! His school reports were always broadly the same, congratulating him on his happy, friendly nature, but bemoaning his academic abilities. Unusually, he had shown one real talent at school, as a cook. The school ran domestic science classes and he excelled. He enjoyed cooking so much that when he left school there was never any intention that he would go to university, he had decided that he would somehow use his cooking skills to make a living. His father came up with a solution. Simon recalled, very clearly, Robert suggesting that he sets up his own catering business. He jumped at the chance, his father gave him some capital to start the business and helped him win a couple of small catering contracts to get him started and he never looked back. The business went from strength to strength and within five years he employed more than fifty staff, he was just twenty-three years old. It was through his business, a few years later, that he met Patricia. She was working for a corporate events company and regularly used his company to provide the catering. They were married within a year of meeting. They experienced difficult times in the years ahead, when it seemed that they would never be able to have the children that they so wanted. They had considered adopting, but just weren't enthusiastic enough about it and dropped the idea. They had both turned forty when Patricia told him that she was expecting. He could still see her face when she told him, they both started crying, but it soon turned to laughter. It was, without doubt, the happiest time of his life so far. Emily was born and they moved into the family home in Hampstead.

Emily was now fast asleep and Patricia had joined Simon in the nursery, where they sat contentedly together on the floor watching her sleep.

Erik Norberg loved living in New York. He had been staying at the *W Hotel* on Union Square, but the HR department of the bank in London that he worked for had called him earlier in the day, to tell him that they had rented a furnished apartment for him in nearby Gramercy Park and he could move in next week. Erik was delighted and was looking forward to going out with some of his colleagues from the bank's office in New York to celebrate. The takeover of the smaller American bank was progressing well and HR in London had also told him during the call that he may well be asked to stay in New York for a further six months. They told him that they needed someone with his experience to not just manage the takeover, but to oversee 'integration', as they described it, following the purchase.

Erik emailed or spoke with his mother in London most days. For as long as he could remember, Julia had been his inspiration in life. As he grew up, she had explained to him what she had gone through in her youth, being abandoned as a baby and taken into care, her subsequent move to London to work as an au pair, falling pregnant and experiencing hardship. Despite all of this, Erik often reminded himself that he had experienced a happy, at times magical childhood, full of caring and love provided by Julia.

106

He was initially unhappy about being sent away to boarding school at such a young age, at first he missed his mother terribly, but he was determined, for her sake, to make it work and to do well. She was still young herself and could enjoy a working career and he not only accepted this as he grew up, but encouraged her.

Erik excelled at school and was accepted at Oxford University, where he got a first class honours degree in English Literature. He took a gap year after Oxford, travelling throughout the Far East and when he returned to London, found a job at the bank where he still worked, in the City, via its graduate training scheme. He rented an apartment in East London with two of the other graduate recruits, who had joined the bank at the same time. He would visit Julia at least once a week, she had moved to a smart new apartment block in Bayswater, where she would soon start her own accountancy business. Erik couldn't have been more proud of his mother and he knew that she felt the same about him.

Erik recognised that his mother was quite a private person and in many ways, he had taken after her in this respect. For as long as he could remember, he'd known that she was a beautiful woman. Tall and slim, with natural blonde hair. He had never known who his father was, it was not something that they discussed, but he had always assumed that he had taken his dark looks from the man whom his mother had fallen pregnant to, following their one night stand. He still vaguely remembered the handsome, kind man, who occasionally took him and his mother to the seaside when he was little. As he got a bit older, perhaps six or seven, he would sometimes see the two of them holding hands and once even kissing, but after he had gone to boarding school he never saw him again. For some reason, that he could not fully explain, he had always felt that his mother's mysterious friend was still somewhere in the background, even after all these years. When he was staying in the flat with her in Bayswater, she would often receive calls on her mobile phone and it was made obvious to him, in a gentle subtle way, that they were private. Quite recently, he had asked her why she had never married, after all, whenever they were out together she would always receive admiring glances from men, some of them younger than him! In response, she had just laughed and told him that she was far too busy with her business. Erik often thought to himself that he would be pleased if she did find a partner to settle down with and he had told her as much.

There was a part of his own life that he had chosen not to share with Julia. Since his late teens, Erik had known that he was gay. It had never been an issue for him and he felt comfortable with his sexuality. He had been lucky, that by studying in Oxford and working his whole life in London and now New York, he had lived in cosmopolitan cities, amongst many diverse people and consequently, had hardly ever experienced discrimination or unpleasantness. He wasn't entirely sure why he had never told his mother, because he was pretty sure that she would be understanding and very supportive. Whilst he had been working in New York, he had been giving the idea of telling her some thought and had finally decided that he would speak to her about it on his next visit to London. Strangely, his mind had been made up following a discussion he had with an older gay man, whom he had met through a mutual friend one evening in a bar in Greenwich Village. Jack, was in his mid-sixties and had built up a very successful business empire throughout Europe and the Far East. In fact, he told Erik that his business was so successful that he rarely worked at all and spent most of his time travelling around the world enjoying himself. As the two of them shared a bottle of wine, Jack revealed that he had been married, but was now divorced. He had raised a family and none of them, nor any of his friends knew, even to this day, that he was a gay man. He said that he only really felt free when he was far from home and could be himself. For some reason, which he couldn't really explain, although afterwards he thought it might have been the wine, Erik told Jack about his own life and the question he was grappling with about whether to tell his mother about his own sexuality. Jack was unequivocal, he must tell her as soon as he can or, he risked ending up like him a wealthy, but at times sad, older man running away from the truth.

CHAPTER FIFTEEN

THE NURSING HOME

Margaret Coleville boarded the Boeing 737 aircraft at Ancona airport for the flight to Stansted. Robert had agreed to meet her there and drive them back to Chelsea. Her stay in Le Marche had been overshadowed by her concerns over the interest the journalist had shown in one of the photographs in the dining room in Hampstead. She was convinced that Peter Wilson had engineered his return to the dining room, on the pretense of forgetting his mobile phone, to get a closer look or, even a photograph of the picture with Simon and his nanny. She remembered his immediate reaction, during dinner, when he first saw the photo. He had that look of surprise which is virtually impossible to suppress when you see something totally unexpected and she had seen it, the raised eyebrows and his instinctive movement forward to try and get a better look. She had replayed the conversation that they had, when she joined him in the dining room later, over and over in her mind. Had she appeared nervous and said too much? She remembered mentioning Tara, the nanny, did she tell him that she had wanted to become a nurse? She couldn't remember, did it matter if she had? Whatever the details of their conversation were, Margaret had gained the distinct impression that he was very interested in that particular photograph. But why? It was a normal family photo of two smiling parents and a nanny holding their newly born son, what on earth could be suspicious about such an innocent picture? There are probably very similar photographs in the homes of middle class families up and down the country,

110

she thought. The only slightly unusual aspect may have been the presence of Tara, the nanny. But how on earth could that have made him look so surprised? She had made her mind up, she would share her suspicions with Robert after all, he was the only other person in the world with whom she could share them!

Isabella had booked the table for dinner in Islington whilst having coffee with Patricia in her kitchen in Hampstead. Emily was in her high chair, looking contented and sleepy after being fed. Isabella had checked with Peter that he was free and Patricia said that Simon would be fine with the arrangements.

Patricia had been pondering over what, if anything, to do about the photographs she had found in the attic. She had looked at the copies she had taken with her mobile phone so many times, that she now knew every picture in detail. The mother and child in the pictures were strangely familiar to her and it was beginning to bother her that she couldn't figure out why. When she first discovered the photographs, she had been prepared to believe that they were simply pictures of one of Robert's constituents and her son that, perhaps, he had been helping. That could explain why they were amongst his constituency files. But if that was the case, why had Robert removed them and taken them with him when he visited the attic after Sunday lunch? In the back of her mind was the uncomfortable thought that perhaps the young blonde woman had been Robert's mistress and the dark haired boy their son. For that reason, she was reluctant to ask Simon, who she would normally share everything with, and she certainly wouldn't ask Margaret or, for that matter, Robert about them. Perhaps the reason she thought the boy in the photograph was familiar to her was because he did look a bit like Robert. But he also looked like someone else that she knew and she couldn't work out who it was. The blonde woman's features were also annoyingly familiar to her and it was driving her mad.

On a happier note, Isabella had been telling her how well her relationship with Peter was progressing. She told her that she felt totally at ease in his company and she believed that he felt the same whenever they were together. Patricia was delighted for her friend. She had known Isabella for a number of years but initially, only as a neighbour of Robert and Margaret. Now that Isabella was her neighbour, they had spent more time together and become close friends. In that Latin way, she was a very open minded person and comfortable sharing with Patricia quite intimate details of her life. Patricia, being English, was naturally a more conservative person, but had warmed to Isabella and felt that she could confide in her. Perhaps she could speak to her about the photographs and ask for her advice? She decided to give it some thought.

The drive from Chelsea to Stansted Airport was surprisingly straightforward and relatively stress free, the traffic was fairly light, helped by the fact that Robert didn't need to leave home until mid-morning, well after the rush hour. He left the car in the short term car park and walked across to the arrivals lounge to meet Margaret. During the drive, Robert had given more thought on what, if anything, to do about Peter Wilson, following his meeting with Julia. There was also the matter of Patricia finding the constituency files, which contained the photographs of Julia and Erik. As he greeted Margaret with a hug and helped her with her luggage, little did he know that he was about to be confronted with another piece of bad news, which would determine his next move.

Robert sensed that Margaret was preoccupied and a little tense when she sat next to him in the car as they started their drive back to Chelsea. Having lived with someone who had

112

suffered bouts of depression for more than forty years, he was very conscious of Margaret's mood swings.

"How was the New Year in Le Marche?" Robert asked.

"It was lovely to spend time with old friends, but I'm glad to be home now, it can be quite grim over there in the countryside at this time of year. I often wonder if we should consider selling and moving to a city, Bologna or Milan perhaps." Margaret replied.

They'd had this conversation many times over the years, the winter months up in the hills of Le Marche could certainly be grim Robert thought, but as soon as they visited the farmhouse during the Spring or Summer or, even in early Autumn, there was nowhere else in the world that they would rather spend their time.

"Before I forget, we really must take the car over to Hampstead soon," Robert said, changing the subject. "Pat found more of our junk up in the attic you know, do you remember all of that bedding and curtain material we left in your father's old trunk up there?" Robert asked, being careful not to mention the other contents of the trunk.

"It's hardly junk Robert!" Margaret replied, sounding more like her old self, "it was all from Harrods and Liberty as far as I can remember."

Robert laughed.

"That reminds me, there is something I want to talk to you about Hampstead Robert," Margaret continued, it's about the night of the dinner party we hosted to celebrate you completing your book."

Robert detected some tension in Margaret's voice.

"Do you remember towards the end of dinner that journalist friend of yours….."

"Peter Wilson." Robert interrupted a little too quickly, he thought afterwards.

"Yes, yes Peter Wilson," she continued slightly agitated, "I am sure that he noticed something that surprised him in one of the photographs on the credenza, the one with you and me, along with that nanny we had for a short while, Tara, holding Simon."

"Surprised?" Robert asked, paying more attention.

"Yes, surprised, as though he had seen something that had, well, kind of shocked him. Anyway, after dinner when we all went into the drawing room he excused himself, saying he had left his phone in the dining room and would pop back in there and get it."

"I don't remember that." Robert said, suddenly sensing danger.

"You were pouring drinks for the other guests at the time." Margaret paused. "The thing is, I followed him back in there after a minute or two and found him looking at that same photograph again."

"What did you say to him?" Robert's tone was suddenly serious.

"Nothing much really, it was the first time I had spoken to him alone and I think I said how sorry I was to hear about his wife or something like that." Margaret was feeling anxious now, it was very rare for them to discuss anything which remotely concerned the events that happened over forty years ago.

"And what did he say about the photograph?" Robert asked.

"I think he just said what lovely pictures they were and I mentioned that we had a nanny at the time to help us get over the shock of having a new born baby in the house, a Persian girl we called her Tara, who wanted to become a nurse. It was the look on his face though Robert, when he first saw the photo over dinner, you can't disguise your reactions to a sudden shock, I'm sure he knows something."

"How can he know something, it was more than forty years ago for Christ's sake." Robert replied sharply. "It's nothing Margaret, forget all about it."

He knew that there was no point in continuing the discussion, but he also knew that Margaret wouldn't forget about it and neither would he. Peter Wilson meeting Julia, Pat possibly discovering the photos taken on Camber sands and now this. The rest of the journey took place in relative silence. Robert had already decided what he had to do next.

The Lavender Gardens Nursing Home in Highgate, North London provided residential care for the elderly. It was one of the best and most expensive nursing homes in London. Robert drove up the gravel drive and left the car in the visitors' car park. As he walked towards the reception area he admired the beautifully kept gardens that, even in February, managed to provide some colour on an overcast afternoon. After providing his details to the receptionist, he was met by the director of nursing, Jillian Tompkins. He had telephoned the day before to inform Miss Tompkins that he would be visiting.

"Please follow me Mr. Coleville and I'll take you up to her room." Miss Tompkins informed him and led the way to a lift, which took them up to the second floor. Robert noticed that the home was tastefully decorated and spotlessly clean, which pleased him. Miss Tompkins knocked gently on the door of room 5 and entered.

"Mrs. Jeffreys, your visitor has arrived, Mr. Coleville."

A very old lady, sat in an armchair by the large bay window, looked up and smiled.

"Robert, what a lovely surprise! Thank you Jillian, would you have the tea sent up when it's ready please." Mrs. Jeffreys asked.

"Of course Mrs. Jeffreys, I'll have it sent up immediately, Mr. Coleville has brought you some beautiful flowers, I'll have them put in water and sent up as well. Just call me if there is anything else you need." Miss Tompkins said and left them alone together.

"Hello Beryl." Robert walked across the room to where she was sitting and gave her a peck on the cheek.

115

"Come and sit down Robert, I'm sorry I can't get up, it's my legs you know, I'll be ninety-three next month!" and she laughed, "is everything alright, Margaret and Simon?"

The old lady looked worried for a moment, expecting some terrible news.

"They're both fine Beryl, everyone is fine." Robert noticed the relief in her face when he told her. "You're happy here Beryl and well looked after? It certainly seems a nice home."

"I love it here Robert, I couldn't manage on my own anymore and I get plenty of visitors, Simon comes and sees me quite often, he's so kind you know." Beryl said slightly tearful, Robert noticed.

Robert was pleased that she was happy and comfortable. Margaret and her family had found the home for Beryl a few years earlier and helped towards the cost of her care.

"You were like a second mother to him Beryl, I don't know what we'd have done without you all those years ago." Robert told her.

"He brought Emily with him to see me one day, she's the spitting image of him you know." she smiled.

A young nurse arrived pushing a trolley containing a pot of tea, a plate of cucumber sandwiches and the flowers in a vase.

"Thank you, they're lovely flowers Robert, would you mind pouring, I've got a bit of arthritis I'm afraid."

Robert poured the tea and put it on the mahogany side table next to Beryl, along with some cucumber sandwiches on a plate.

"I won't pretend that the reason I've come here is purely a social visit Beryl, there's something I want, it's your memory." Robert told her, whilst gazing out of the bay window at the gardens.

"You always were honest Robert, straight to the point that was you, most unlike a politician." Robert turned

116

around to face Beryl and laughed, remembering that she always did have a sharp sense of humour.

"And you always knew everything that went on in the house Beryl!" Robert replied.

"How can I help you Robert?" Beryl asked.

"When Margaret came home from the hospital with Simon, we quickly arranged for a nanny to come and help out. I had a contact at the Iranian Embassy at the time and his young daughter was looking for a job. He was working with me on a defence contract for his country and he mentioned to me that she was at a loose end, if anything cropped up. Do you remember her Beryl?"

"Yes......yes I do Robert, her name was Taraneh, Taraneh Saderzadeh, a lovely girl, I'd never met anyone from Persia before. When Simon was sleeping she used to come and help me in the kitchen. She dreamed of becoming a nurse and when the opportunity arose, she jumped at the chance."

"Is that why she left us?" Robert asked.

"Yes, she got offered a job to train as a nurse at a famous hospital in Oxford, the Radcliffe Infirmary, I remember the name of it clearly to this day because a nephew of mine was born at the hospital before the war and I went and visited him there. We kept in touch you know Robert for quite a few years after she left us. She would write to me from Oxford at Christmas and on my birthday and I would write back to her."

"Are you still in touch with her Beryl?" Robert asked

"No…no, not any more, the last letter I received from her came from Persia, her father had to go home she said and she went back with him. It was the end of 1978, I remember the light blue airmail letter, I still have it somewhere, there was trouble in Persia, a revolution I think. She married in Oxford you know, but sadly it ended quite quickly in divorce, she told me in one of her letters, he was

117

a doctor I think, yes he was a doctor. Can I ask you why you want to know about her Robert?" Beryl asked.

Robert was looking at the old lady intently.

"Did Taraneh ever speak to you about Simon and ask you about his birth or, perhaps something she'd overheard in the house about him?" Robert asked and for some reason he got the impression that Beryl had been waiting for this question.

"You'd been entertaining, a dinner party I think and the following morning Taraneh came to help me clear up in the kitchen. Margaret had taken Simon for a walk, it must have been a Saturday or Sunday, because you were driving down to the constituency in Sussex. I could tell she was bit upset about something, she was very quiet which was unusual for her and I asked her what the matter was. She said something about an argument she'd overheard during the night and then straight out of the blue, she asked me whether Simon was really yours and Margaret's child."

Robert felt himself sweating and wiped his forehead with his handkerchief.

"And what did you say to her Beryl?"

"I told her not to be so silly and asked her where she could have got such an idea. I remember she looked a bit embarrassed and went red in the face and said that she had made a mistake and she must have had a bad dream." Beryl paused and turned to the side in her armchair to see Robert staring out of the window, he looked as if he'd seen a ghost, she thought, "I hope everything is alright Robert, it is isn't it?"

"Yes, everything is fine Beryl," Robert had composed himself and turned around to face her, "everything is just fine."

When Robert got back home to Chelsea, he immediately turned on his laptop and typed into the *Google* search engine '*Peter Wilson journalist biography*'. He opened the *Wikipedia* entry for Peter Wilson, English journalist and just as he thought, his career started as a reporter in Oxford for the Oxford Mail between 1972 and 1974.

CHAPTER SIXTEEN

PLATE SPINNING

Isabella lay in Peter's arms. They were both relieved that it had been gentle and felt natural and even more, that they both felt confident enough to discuss their obvious relief with each other. The dinner in Islington with Simon and Patricia had been fun and all four of them had probably drank more than they should have done, particularly Patricia. Following dinner, the four of them had shared a taxi back to Hampstead. Simon and Patricia were dropped off first, Margaret had been babysitting Emily for them and consequently, they felt that they could fully relax on their first night out together for some time. Isabella had asked Peter in for coffee when the taxi stopped outside her house. They never drank the coffee which she made and here they were in bed together, both blissfully happy.

"We should try and sleep Peter, it's nearly two a.m." Isabella sighed.

"Yes, we should, you know what struck me tonight about Pat and Simon, is how happy and content they are in each other's company." Peter said.

"Like us you mean!" Isabella laughed.

"Yes of course," Peter added quickly, "but I've rarely seen a couple married for as long as them to be so close, it's quite endearing, I get the impression they are very dependent upon one another, a real partnership, what do you think?"

Isabella was really thinking about whether Peter had been that happy with Gloria. He'd told her once before that they had a very happy marriage, but she didn't feel it was the right time to ask about her again, certainly not tonight anyway.

"I know Pat a lot better than I know Simon, but I agree yes, they are very well suited to each other and share almost everything, although Pat did bring up something quite strange with me just before we left the restaurant." Isabella said sitting up in bed.

"I'm not sure you should be telling me this, is it a woman's thing?" Peter joked.

"Not really," and Isabella was suddenly quite serious, "I don't think she would have told me if she'd been sober you know, it was when we were waiting for the taxi and you and Simon had gone to stand by the door to make sure nobody else grabbed it. She told me that she had stumbled upon some old photographs, from the nineteen-seventies I think she said, amongst Robert's files that he'd left in the attic in Hampstead. She said that some of them looked like typical family photos taken at the seaside. They were of a young beautiful blonde woman and a small boy, presumably her child. The boy was building sandcastles on a beach somewhere in Sussex, she told me the name of the place but I've forgotten it."

"How did she know the name of the place?" Peter asked becoming interested in Isabella's story.

"She said the name of the place was written on the back of the photos, anyway there were a couple of other pictures of the same young, dark haired, boy in a new school uniform. These ones were taken a few years later and she said the boy looked as though he was about seven or eight in these ones. Pat seems to be convinced that the young woman and the boy are something to do with Robert and its unsettled her." Isabella told him.

"What makes her think that?" Peter asked. "There could be an entirely innocent explanation for the pictures."

"Well, apparently, when Pat told him that he'd left some of his files up in the attic, she obviously didn't mention the photos she'd seen, he went up there to have a look and now the photos are missing."

"You mean, Robert just took the photos but left the files up there?"

"Exactly! He said he'd take the files next time he brought the car to Hampstead. Pat went up in the attic the next morning and the photos were gone though. Something else Pat told me, which is the really odd thing though, is that she feels that the woman and boy in the photos are somehow familiar to her."

Peter had also sat up in bed now and suddenly felt wide awake.

"What, as if they look like some other people she knows?" he asked.

"Yes, I think so, but she said she's been thinking about it so much and can't think who and it's beginning to drive her mad."

"What did you say to her?" Peter asked.

"I could tell that she was, well, worried about it really, I got the impression that she feels that there are some skeletons in the cupboard which might disturb her life with Simon and Emily and she hasn't got anyone to talk to about it. She said she won't talk to Simon about it….anyway, I told her not to worry and to call me if she wants to talk about it further with me." Isabella replied.

She turned off the bedside lamp and they lay contentedly in bed together. Peter's mind had wondered though, the young beautiful blonde in the photographs that Patricia had discovered was Julia Norberg and the young dark haired boy was Robert and Margaret's child, he was pretty sure of that. What he didn't understand though, was how Sir Robert Coleville had come to be in possession of the photos in the first place.

Robert Coleville sat quietly in his kitchen in Chelsea having breakfast. Margaret had spent the night in

122

Hampstead, where she had babysat Emily. She had told Robert before she left for Hampstead that Simon and Patricia were going out for dinner in Islington with Peter Wilson and Isabella who, according to Patricia, were now "an item". Robert didn't react when she told him, the last thing he needed was Margaret becoming even more anxious and doing something stupid. What he really needed was more time. More time to think and consider whether any of the recent incidents were related or, just a series of coincidences. Peter Wilson seeing the photograph of Taraneh Saderzadeh and now making contact with Julia and then Pat finding the photographs of Julia and Erik in the attic.

He thought to himself how, against all the odds, he had managed to keep everything under control for more than forty years. There had been extremely difficult times during this period, when he had sometimes felt like one of those circus performers that they used to show on black and white television, spinning dozens of plates on thin poles and preventing any of them from falling to the ground. Until recently, he had been confident that no one had any suspicions that Margaret had brought Julia Norberg's baby home from the maternity hospital all those years ago. Oddly enough, as time passed following that terrible day, his main concern was not that somebody would find out what she had done, that was highly unlikely after all, who would ever suspect a respectable middle-class MP's wife of abduction? No, his main concern had been keeping his long term relationship with Julia, he hated the term affair, a secret not only from Margaret, but from anyone else he knew. For a number of years he had deliberately cultivated the image that he was a ladies man which, in reality, couldn't have been further from the truth. He would go to great lengths to let Margaret assume that he was having the occasional affair, letting her discover evidence, that he had concocted himself, of his infidelity with different women. None of these affairs actually happened, but it diverted Margaret away from the truth, that he was in a long term relationship with Julia, the woman who was raising their real child. God only knows what Margaret would do if she ever discovered that her son was alive and well and virtually running a bank! It didn't bear thinking about.

Looking back, it was quite easy all those years ago to find out that their son was alive and just as easy to trace where the woman, who took him home believing he was her son, lived. That her home at the time was no more than a ten minute walk from his own home in Hampstead was remarkable. Ridiculous, he remembers thinking at the time! Well, they say truth can be stranger than fiction, well it certainly was in Robert Coleville's world, he thought to himself.

Befriending Julia when she worked at the library was not easy though. It still made him feel wretched, even today, that he deliberately struck up a relationship with her for the sole aim of making sure that his son was well cared for and healthy and to help him in any way he could. All this, without Julia knowing. The only consolation he could find at the time was that he had been totally honest with her about the rest of his life, that he was a married MP with a young child called Simon, who had no intention of leaving his wife. The risks were enormous, Julia could have blown everything sky-high at any moment. Strangely enough, telling her the truth about the rest of his life was probably the best thing he ever did because, as time passed, she seemed to accept his other life and of course, her overriding priority, which she often told him, was to provide for her son in a way that she had never experienced during her young life.

The easiest and most unexpected aspect of the whole episode was falling in love with Julia. He now realised that it was this love, which was eventually reciprocated, that had kept him sane all these years. He often thought to himself, what would have happened if we hadn't fallen in love? Like Margaret finding out one day that her real son was alive and well or, Julia discovering that she had been deceived and had brought up another mother's son and was now a grandmother to a beautiful little girl called Emily, it really didn't bear thinking about. And now, after coping with all of this for more than forty years, he felt that his life was on the brink of falling apart again, it just seemed so unfair. It was happening quickly as well, evidence coming at him from all directions.

There were lots of 'what ifs', Robert thought to himself. What if, he hadn't bumped into Peter Wilson at that dinner at the Savoy or, asked him to help him with his memoirs? Even that wouldn't have mattered if he hadn't invited him to dinner in Hampstead. He wouldn't have seen that bloody photograph on the credenza and remembered Taraneh from their days in Oxford. She must have told him the same story that she told Beryl about hearing the argument. He had no actual proof that they had known each other in Oxford but, as they say, the circumstantial evidence was compelling. What if, he hadn't been careless and left the seaside photos in the attic? What will Pat do if she has seen them? There was no doubt in Robert's mind that Peter Wilson was on to him, he'd even met Julia. How on earth did he find out about her? Wilson knew the truth or, had a good idea of the truth, he was a renowned investigative journalist for Christ's sake, of course he would get to the bottom of it eventually, and then what?

Peter shared a leisurely breakfast with Isabella before returning home to Marylebone later in the morning. As soon as he got in, he logged on using his laptop to check his emails and there, at the top of his inbox, was one from Julia Norberg Accountancy Limited. He opened the email and read a business-like, but polite message, telling him that a quote was attached and she hoped to hear from him in the near future. Peter opened the attached file, which was in PDF format and whilst the amount she was proposing to charge him for looking after his company accounts was really irrelevant, he noted that it seemed very reasonable. His overall impression of Julia was that she was a very professional business woman.

Peter sat back in his office chair and reflected on what he knew so far. Simon is Julia Norberg's real son he thought. Julia unwittingly took home Robert's and Margaret's son from the maternity hospital and from what Isabella had told him earlier that morning regarding the photographs Patricia had discovered, Julia had brought up the boy. It certainly looked that way, from Isabella's description of the photos. Two important questions remained unanswered though. Where is the child in the photographs now? According to Isabella, he was about seven or eight years old in some of them. But more importantly, why is Robert in possession of the photographs? Did he take them without Julia knowing? Possibly those taken on the beach, but the ones of the boy in school uniform, unlikely he thought. So, perhaps Robert knew Julia back then and maybe, just maybe, he is still in touch with her. It was an incredible thought!

Two things were worrying Peter as he considered what to do next. Firstly, Isabella. He felt slightly guilty and worried that, at some point in the future he could be accused that he had only become close to her because she was a friend of the Coleville's. He knew that nothing could be further from the truth, but it did leave a nasty taste in the mouth. It was the first intimate relationship he'd had since Gloria died and he felt happy about it and the last thing he wanted was for it to be ruined. He certainly couldn't tell Isabella anything about his investigations. If he was to be accused at some time in the future of deceiving her, he decided to cross that bridge, if and when he came to it.

The other issue that was worrying him was much more complex, a moral issue really, he thought. As far as he knew, everyone involved in this mystery, certainly those that had played no part in the deception and were blameless are, on the face of it, leading happy lives. He thought of Simon and Patricia and of course, Emily. A lovely family who would naturally be devastated if they ever found out the truth. Peter knew through his experience as an investigative journalist that, when faced with unpleasant truths, it is often unpredictable how innocent party's caught up in events will react. Sometimes, as they say, ignorance is bliss. Although he was less sure of Julia Norberg's role in the whole affair, she seemed to be a smart, hard working woman who, for all he knew, had brought up a son who would now be in his early forties, completely unaware of the fact that he was not her real son. Peter shuddered at the thought of the damage that would be caused to these two families, should Robert and Margaret Coleville's deceit be exposed. He was convinced that Margaret had deliberately taken Julia's son home from the hospital and along with Robert, had hidden the crime for more than forty years. It still wasn't clear why Margaret had done this, but some kind of mental breakdown and a morbid fear that her real son may not live long were possibilities, he thought. He remembered reading about a woman many years ago who had lost two daughters during childbirth and had committed a similar crime, following years of depression and mental illness. Robert's role in the deceit was still confusing, but through the photographs Patricia had discovered there was now a definite link between him and Julia Norberg, the woman who had brought up his son. Could he possibly of been having a long term relationship with Julia, to somehow remain close to his son? Peter suddenly felt very angry with Robert Coleville and decided to find out how he came to be in possession of the photographs. He re-opened the email from Julia Norberg Accountancy Limited and replied, accepting the quotation, and requested a meeting at her office in Bayswater, so that he could deliver documents relating to the previous tax year, which would soon need her attention. He then rang Mathew and arranged to meet him for lunch the following day at *The Elephant and Castle*.

CHAPTER SEVENTEEN

OUR SECRET

Margaret's parents were delighted when Robert proposed to her. He was exactly the sort of "chap" that they hoped their only daughter would marry. At the time, Robert was working at Conservative Central Office and lived in the beautiful house in Hampstead, which had been left to him by his parents when they moved to Golder's Green. Brigadier Pennington and his wife, Rosemary, had been slightly worried that their daughter might struggle to find someone suitable to marry. Whilst she was a highly intelligent and attractive young woman, she had suffered from bouts of depression even at a relatively young age and naturally they were pleased that she had found such an eligible young man. Robert's parents had both died by this time and Margaret conveniently glossed over exactly how they had made their money in the rag trade in East London.

The wedding was a grand affair in the Hampshire village where Margaret was born. She remembered the large number of local dignitaries who had attended, her family were part of what was then often described as the County set. Robert would often tease her about her background, where everyone seemed to wear tweed all year round. It was Robert's non-conformity and slightly rakish side that attracted Margaret to him in the first place. At university, where they met, he rarely mixed with the upper class students, unless it concerned politics and had very little to do with the sporty crowd, who played rugby and rowed. However, he was extremely handsome and tall, with dark wavy hair and dark eyes. Margaret's girlfriends often told her that he looked like a matinee idol, which amused her.

He was also wealthy. The house in Hampstead was worth a small fortune and by the time they married, he had already inherited his parent's house in Golder's Green, as well a large portfolio of stocks and shares in largely blue chip companies. Robert subsequently used some of his inheritance to purchase the country cottage in Sussex, when he became an MP in 1970, just two years after their marriage. Looking back, Margaret came to the conclusion that, sadly, this was almost certainly the high point of their long life together, they really did feel, for a short time, that they had the world at their feet. Robert was even being tipped as a future leader of the Conservative Party. Margaret smiled when she remembered being photographed for one or two of the Sunday newspapers', newly launched, colour supplements. When she fell pregnant for the first time they were both overjoyed and although, at times, she felt some anxiety, which she tended to keep to herself, it was a very happy time for both of them.

Margaret's miscarriage came as a terrible shock for them, but particularly for Margaret. Until then, pretty much everything in life had come easily to her and she struggled to come to terms with the loss. Robert was sympathetic and told her that it was just one of those terrible things that happen in life and constantly reminded her that the doctors had told them that there was no underlying problem, which would stop them having children in the future. When she fell pregnant again, later that year and the baby was stillborn seven months into the pregnancy, Margaret slipped quickly into depression. Now, more than forty years later, she had a much clearer picture of what was happening to her during those terrible weeks and months, following the stillbirth of her child. At the time, she had little idea what was going on in her body either physically or mentally, it was just frightening. Whilst Robert was kind and supportive, they would talk for hours some evenings before drifting off to sleep, he was also incredibly busy as an MP, particularly since his recent appointment as a junior minister. Margaret had felt terribly alone and at times, scared. Her parents had no idea how to deal with her illness and on one occasion she remembered her mother, Rosemary, losing her temper and telling her to pull herself together. Mrs Jeffreys, the housekeeper, who had worked for the Penningtons in Hampshire before joining them in Hampstead, was more of a mother to her during this period. Always kind and full of common sense, was the way Robert used to describe her.

When Margaret fell pregnant for the third and final time she was terrified that she would lose yet another child. She had been taking anti-depressants since the stillbirth and looking back years later, she recognised that that these drugs were really in their infancy in those days and some of the side effects were unknown. On the face of it, the pregnancy went well. She experienced very little morning sickness and the weight she gained during pregnancy made her look much healthier than she had done for some time, she had lost a lot of weight beforehand and had become painfully thin during the past year. Once again, looking back, Margaret remembered very little of the actual birth. In fact, it was very straightforward but, because her son was slightly jaundiced when he was born, purely as a precaution, he was taken away from her and treated in an incubator in an adjoining room in the maternity hospital. Margaret panicked during the night, convinced that her baby was not going to survive. She remembered hearing voices telling her that she must take a healthy baby home. In the early hours of the morning she went into the adjoining room and saw two incubators, with a baby in each. The young blonde girl, who had shared the ward with her, had also given birth to a boy the previous afternoon and her baby had also been placed in an incubator. Margaret hadn't seen the attractive blonde girl since she was taken to the theatre to give birth, which had puzzled her. In a state of high anxiety and with

131

voices in her head driving her on, Margaret switched the tags on the babies' ankles and then switched the two babies in the incubators. It had been surprisingly easy she thought as she returned to the empty ward and got back into bed. It was as though a huge weight had been lifted off her, the voices in her head stopped, she felt relaxed and she drifted off to sleep, through sheer exhaustion.

The next morning the nurse returned the baby to Margaret and she was told that the doctor had said there was no more need for any special treatment or observation. Margaret was surprised, but relieved that she would soon be going home with a healthy baby boy. Robert and her parents visited her that morning and plans were made for her to return home. Margaret was insistent that she felt fine and wanted to go home as soon as possible and the hospital staff saw no reason why she shouldn't. Before leaving, she noticed that the young blonde girl had still not returned to the ward. Margaret remembered her as a beautiful girl with blue/grey eyes and felt a bit sorry for her that she had received no visitors during their stay on the ward. They had probably only spoken once or twice, Margaret didn't even know her name.

The enormity of what she had done did not hit Margaret until she returned home and spoke with Robert. Mrs. Jeffreys took care of the baby almost immediately. Robert and Margaret had arranged for a full time, live-in, nanny to start work and she would be arriving later in the week. Margaret told Robert what she had done as soon as they were alone in their bedroom. Oddly, she felt quite relaxed about it and even thought that Robert might be pleased at her quick thinking in the maternity hospital, when it became clear to her that her own son was not going to live. She soon realised that this was not the case, Robert was horrified. She remembered him just staring at her, for what seemed like an eternity, but was probably only a matter of seconds. Then, he did something that she had never seen him do before and had never seen him do since, he started to cry. Sobbing would be a more accurate description. When, after a few minutes, he had composed himself he took control of the situation. He told her to stay in the bedroom and say nothing to anyone. He then went out, Margaret recalled hearing the car on the gravel drive and it was at least two hours before he returned home. Years later, he told her that he had driven to the Jewish cemetery in Golder's Green and sat next to his father's grave and asked him for advice.

Whatever advice he had received from his deceased father, when he returned home he was a different man to the one Margaret had last seen a few hours earlier. Even after all these years, Margaret could remember, virtually word for word, what he had said to her on his return from the cemetery.

"You must never mention what happened in the hospital to anyone other than me, ever. It will be our secret Margaret, if we keep this secret between ourselves no one will ever find out the truth. No one in their right mind would ever suspect an MP's wife of such an act, I know you understand me Margaret, it will be our secret."

Looking back, Margaret thought that had she been in her right mind, she would never have committed such a terrible act, as Robert had described it, in the first place. She now understood she had been very sick and had probably suffered some kind of nervous breakdown.

Her anxiety came and went during the first twenty four hours following her return home. Remarkably, she returned to work on a part time basis, at the university where she worked as a scientist, within days of returning home. Robert had encouraged her, saying that getting back into some kind of normal routine would be for the best. He was probably right, she now thought, days turned into weeks and weeks into months and it became clear that "our secret", as Robert had described it, had not been discovered. Over the years, Margaret often thought back to this period of her life and sometimes couldn't help being impressed at how strong Robert had been throughout the ordeal. On other occasions, she just thought that it was really weakness and he only decided to be complicit in such a dreadful crime to prevent it ruining his career. Either way, as time passed she would remind herself that they had made a pact and she had decided to keep her side of the bargain, come what may.

Over the months and years that followed, Margaret came to love Simon, he was a very loveable child and grew into a very likeable adult and now she had a beautiful granddaughter, Emily. However, rarely had a day passed since she brought Simon home that she hadn't wondered what became of her own son. During the first few weeks, she had even considered trying to find out what happened to the young blonde girl and the baby she had left in the hospital. She remembered mentioning it to Robert one day and he was furious and told her to put all such thoughts out of her mind. She also remembered arguing with him after some dreadful dinner party, when she had threatened to go to the police and tell them the truth. He advised her to forget all about it in no uncertain terms. She soon forgot about it though, she'd caused enough heartache and decided to follow his advice.

As the years passed her relationship with Robert drifted apart, although she dutifully played the part of the MP's wife. She found evidence at home of his infidelity and was initially shocked at just how careless he had become, it was almost as if he wanted her to discover that he was having affairs. She found subtle ways of letting him know, that she knew, without actually confronting him. It almost became a game between them. Interestingly, as she grew older she came to realise that his complicity in their secret made him as guilty as she was, possibly more, bearing in mind she was sick at the time. The secret or, "our secret" as she always thought of it, bound them together, perhaps for the rest of their lives. They had a hold over each other and they both knew the consequences, should either of them do something rash that would result in the truth being discovered.

It was in the early nineteen-nineties, nearly twenty years after they brought Simon home, that they bought the farmhouse in Le Marche. Margaret fell in love with Italy. At last, she had found a place where she could forget her past and feel alive again, almost like a different person. Although it was only a two hour flight away, it felt like total freedom for her, an escape. She was quite happy there on her own, pottering around in the garden, swimming in the pool, cooking Italian recipes. Robert would join her there occasionally and they shared some happy times together, but she knew that deep down he preferred England, particularly Hampstead, the House of Commons, his club in St. James and Sussex.

On her tube journey back to Chelsea, following her babysitting duties, Margaret reflected on her concerns regarding Peter Wilson. She was sure that he was suspicious. He had taken an unusually keen interest in the photograph on the credenza and she didn't fully understand why. She felt less concerned now that she had spoken with Robert about it though. She felt sure that he would sort it out.

Peter arrived at *The Elephant and Castle* before Mathew. He was keen to talk through his plans with his old friend and ask for his opinion, which he regarded highly. Once settled with a pint of bitter each and their food orders placed, Peter told Mathew what Isabella had said about Patricia's discovery in the attic.

"That puts a completely new complexion on the mystery old boy," Mathew commented, "from what you've been told about these photographs, it looks as though they may well have been taken by Robert Coleville and if that is the case, I think we can safely assume that he has had some kind of relationship with Julia Norberg in the past. If he has, then he took an enormous risk and must have had a very good reason for doing so. An attempt to keep in touch with his real son perhaps?"

"Exactly what I've been thinking Matt and maybe his relationship with her is still going on today," Peter added, "took some nerve, I'll say that for him, I wonder what Margaret would do if she ever found out?"

"Perhaps she knew what he was doing all the time and they cooked it up between themselves as a way of making sure the boy was alright, stranger things have happened." Mathew suggested.

"That's very Machiavellian," Peter smiled, "I hadn't thought of that. I'm going to see Julia Norberg again, but at her home in Bayswater, which she also uses as her office. I received her quote by email and I've told her I'd like to proceed."

"I think you should be careful Peter. Sir Robert Coleville has a lot to lose if his secret is ever exposed, not to mention the catastrophic effect it would have on Simon and Patricia, and then there's Julia Norberg and her son."

"Thanks for the advice Matt, it has already crossed my mind that if he is still in touch with Julia, which is what I'm trying to find out, he may already know that I've met her."

"Exactly, old boy, you be careful!" Mathew agreed, looking serious.

Robert had learnt an important lesson during his years as an MP. When faced with a difficult problem, avoid making a decision until there are absolutely no other options open to you. More often than not, doing nothing, turned out to be the best option. His experience had told him that problems often resolved themselves and taking some kind of action could sometimes make the problem worse. This approach had served him well during his years as a politician and strangely enough, he now faced the biggest problem of his life and was tempted to do nothing.

He had never reached the starry heights in his political career, but he was known as a safe pair of hands and as he grew older, ministers would come to him for advice on a variety of subjects. It was the secret he shared with Margaret that had stopped him pursuing high office, which naturally comes with increased scrutiny of your private life and that was the last thing he needed. He had been offered cabinet positions on two occasions, but managed to find believable excuses for turning both jobs down. Over the years he became respected for his integrity and honesty in Tory circles and towards the end of his career as an MP, in 2010, he was knighted for services to the Conservative Party. He was offered a place in the House of Lords, but turned it down, he'd really had enough of it all by then. Writing his memoirs was an unusual step for a politician who had never known high office, but he would be positioning the book as the insider's story, someone who had been very close to many important national and international issues in a career stretching back to the late nineteen-sixties.

Apart from a chapter about growing up in London with parents who had been second generation immigrants and worked in the rag trade, for obvious reasons, there was very little in the book about his personal life. Throughout his life, thinking about his parents always gave Robert courage and drawing on that, along with the lessons he learnt as an MP, he had decided to sit tight and do nothing about the dark clouds closing in on him. If Peter Wilson has proof of any wrongdoing in his past he thought to himself, then let him put up or, shut up!

CHAPTER EIGHTEEN

BETRAYAL

It was a bright, early Spring day and Peter decided to walk to Bayswater for his meeting with Julia Norberg. Oxford Street was busy with shoppers and he was glad when he'd crossed Marble Arch onto the Bayswater Road and left the crowds behind him. He had brought various papers with him relating to his company, along with details of his recent tax returns. He found the apartment block easily and the porter directed him to the lift and told him to exit on the third floor. The porter had obviously called Julia to tell her she had a visitor, because she was waiting at the door for him.

Probably because they had already met, he could sense that she was more relaxed than she had been when they first met in the hotel and she invited him into the lounge for a coffee, before they would go into her office to run through the papers he had brought with him. It was a very smart apartment and the lounge décor definitely had a minimalist Scandinavian feel about it. Peter made himself comfortable, whilst Julia prepared the coffee. He had already spotted the framed photographs on a side table when he came into the room and now he took the opportunity to take a closer look. Both pictures were of the same young man, dressed in a smart business suit. He had dark wavy hair, dark eyes and was extremely handsome. There was no doubt in Peter's mind, it was Robert and Margaret Coleville's son in the photographs. Julia returned and they made some small talk, whilst enjoying the coffee. Peter had expected to find photographs of the Coleville's son in the apartment but, what he was really hoping to find was some sort of evidence that Robert, himself, had visited the apartment. He wasn't to be disappointed. When they had finished their drinks they went into the office, which was surprisingly spacious. Julia sat behind her desk and switched on the desktop computer, whilst Peter took the papers and tax returns out of his shoulder bag and placed them on the desk in front of him. Julia had used the space in the office really well he thought, there were two filing cabinets next to the wall to his left and on his right a printer/photocopier. His attention was caught though when he looked behind where Julia was sat. Two shelves covered the width of the wall behind her, containing box files. Peter scanned the names and dates on each of the spines of the box files, whilst Julia continued logging into the system on the desktop computer. The names on the spines were clearly her clients, organised in alphabetical order by the look of things and it didn't take him long to find the name he was looking for. There were three files, dated '1998-2003', '2004-2009' and '2010-', and each one was labelled Coleville. Julia Norberg was Robert Coleville's accountant. What wonderful cover Coleville had created for himself, Peter thought.

As the meeting came to an end, Peter asked Julia whether she had been an accountant all of her working life.

"Oh no," she replied smiling, "only since 1997, I spent nearly fifteen years working in the House of Commons and then for a bank in the City, before I qualified."

If Peter had stayed an hour longer at Julia's apartment he would have bumped into Sir Robert Coleville. Margaret had left for Italy with Simon, Patricia and Emily the day before and Robert was looking forward to having a late lunch with Julia. She was in a good mood when he arrived and they embraced warmly.

"I'll put the kettle on my love." She told him as he settled down in the lounge, where he noticed the cups and saucers.

"You've had a visitor I see." Robert called after her.

"Yes, new client, that journalist chap I told you about, Peter Wilson." she replied.

It was just as well that Julia was in the kitchen and couldn't see him, he'd gone as white as a sheet. He was sat in the armchair next to the side table, with the framed photographs of Erik on it and he just stared at them. He got up and took the cups and saucers into the kitchen and sat down to drink his tea, whilst Julia prepared lunch.

"Thanks love." she put the cups and saucers in the dishwasher. "He seems like a nice guy, he's left some papers and tax returns for me in the office and I promised I'd look through them in the next day or two. You must have come across him years ago, he was a defence correspondent for a couple of the broadsheets around the time you were at the MoD."

"The name rings a bell, such a long time ago though darling, I prefer to forget about it all to be honest." Robert lied, but his mind had already wondered and he imagined where Peter Wilson would have sat in the office and the view he would have had of the shelves behind Julia's desk. He'd sat there himself from time to time over the past fifteen years and knew exactly what Wilson would have seen on the shelves.

The moment the Ryanair flight landed at Ancona airport Margaret felt she could relax. She found herself spending more and more time in Italy as the years passed and found it therapeutic. She could forget her tortured past in Italy and would sometimes go for days without even thinking of the dreadful events that happened all those years ago in London. It was the guilt that caused her the most pain, that, and having no one other than Robert to discuss it with. Being in Italy provided a release for her and she enjoyed the very ordinary day-to-day tasks, cooking, tending to the garden, shopping in the local markets and walking in the beautiful

Le Marche countryside. Having Simon, Patricia and especially Emily with her on this trip was a bonus. They would be staying for just a week and then afterwards Robert would join her for a few days. She rarely booked a return ticket to Stansted these days and just decided to return to London whenever she felt like it or, if there was some special event to attend, a wedding say or, more likely these days a funeral she thought to herself gloomily. Margaret always called their neighbour, Maurizio, a day or two before she arrived at the farmhouse and as well as tending to the swimming pool, he would air out the rooms and even shop for a few groceries to tide them over until she visited Jesi, the nearest town, to do a proper shop. Maurizio was a godsend, he was what once was described as a handyman and was a great help. He was in his fifties and had no regular employment, but managed to eke out a living by doing odd jobs in the local area, as well as running a stall once a week at the market in nearby Osimo. Margaret was always careful to make sure he was well rewarded, financially, for the help he gave her, so the arrangement worked well for both of them. The weather was unusually warm for March and Simon would be able to use the swimming pool each day, which would please him. Margaret was planning to cook a number of local dishes whilst the family was staying with her and on her previous visit, in January, she had even taken an Italian cooking course in Ancona. Emily was walking now and Margaret had spoken with Patricia about the extra care they would have to take with her, particularly around the pool and inside the old farmhouse. The four of them spent an idyllic week in Italy, it was warm and sunny virtually every day. They ate lunch in the garden most days, Margaret mainly cooked fish and they would enjoy a bottle of Verdicchio, the local white wine from Jesi, with their lunch.

Simon and Patricia were having a swim in the pool on their last full day at the farmhouse, when Margaret called through the kitchen window to them asking if they'd seen her mobile phone anywhere, she'd been looking everywhere for it and wanted to call Robert to tell him what time to pick Simon, Patricia and Emily up, when they arrived back at Stansted Airport the following day.

"My phone is in the kitchen Margaret, just use that if you like, the password's Emily's birthday." Patricia replied.

The moment she had said it, she realised she had made a terrible mistake. She struggled out of the pool, wrapped a towel around herself and headed for the kitchen still soaking wet. When she opened the kitchen door and saw Margaret, she knew she was too late. Margaret was stood looking at Patricia's phone with a horrified look on her face. Patricia felt physically sick, she remembered too late that the last time she had used her phone she had been looking at the photos she'd found in the attic and had left the photo page open. Margaret was looking through the photographs stony-faced.

"Where did get these photos from Pat?" Margaret asked and there was something about the way she looked at her, that left Patricia in no doubt that she must tell her the truth.

"In the attic Margaret, they were in one of Robert's constituency files, I'm so sorry." Patricia was close to tears, but stumbled on, "I have no idea why I took copies of them, I shouldn't have done that, it was unforgivable, but I thought…..I thought I recognised the young woman and child, they looked familiar to me."

"Where are the original photos Pat?" Margaret asked.

"Robert took them, I don't know whether he knows that I've seen them." Particia sat down on one of the kitchen chairs, she felt awful.

"Robert wasn't perfect Pat." Margaret had composed herself by this time, "He had an affair you know, we were going through a difficult patch and it was all over a long time ago, it happens in life. You must never mention what has happened this morning to anyone, not to Simon, not to Robert, not to anyone, do you understand Pat?"

"Yes, of course, I'm so sorry." Patricia could feel herself shaking.

You need to forget all about these pictures, would you like me to delete them for you?" Margaret asked, although Patricia could tell it was more of a statement than a question.

"Yes, please Margaret, I am so sorry."

Margaret deleted the photos, but not before she had forwarded them to her own mobile phone, using WhatsApp and then deleted the WhatsApp chat with Patricia. She went over to where Patricia was sitting and gave her a hug, smiling.

"Let's have lunch, shall we, will you lay the table in the garden please Pat." Margaret told her.

Margaret knew exactly who the young blonde woman was in the photographs, she remembered her from the maternity hospital, even after forty years. How could she ever forget her! She also knew that the young boy in the photos was her own son. He looked so much like Robert. The moment she had seen them, she knew she had been betrayed.

CHAPTER NINETEEN

GLORIA

Peter was travelling by tube to meet Mathew in *The Elephant and Castle*. He was thinking about Robert and Margaret Coleville and was now sure in his own mind that they had deliberately abducted Julia Norberg's new born baby and brought up Simon, as if he was their own child. He was not sure of Robert Coleville's involvement with the actual abduction, but believed that he was complicit in the deception. He was also sure that, unwittingly, Julia Norberg had brought up the Coleville's son, believing that he was her own child and as well as that he was now fairly certain that Robert Coleville had been in some kind of a relationship with Julia for the best part of forty years. The photographs in Patricia's attic indicated that he was in a relationship with her in the nineteen-seventies and Peter now knew that Julia had been his accountant for the past seventeen years. He was not sure of the exact reason behind Robert's relationship with Julia, but felt that it was probably a means of him ensuring that he kept some kind of link to his real son. Peter was also confident that Julia knew nothing of the Coleville's deception. He was unsure of whether Margaret was aware of Robert's relationship with Julia, but felt it was very unlikely. Whilst the Coleville's daughter-in-law, Patricia, had found the photographs in her attic, possibly providing proof of Robert's deception, he was pretty sure that she was unaware of the terrible truth and probably thought it was merely evidence of an extramarital affair Robert had many years ago. Patricia may

144

even be thinking that the child in the photos was a result of his relationship with Julia.

In contrast with all this deception and confusion, Peter couldn't help thinking of his own relationship with his wife, Gloria. They had met in nineteen-eighty and Peter smiled when he remembered that it was his old friend Mathew who had introduced him to Gloria. He had arranged a blind date for the two of them. Mathew had been dating one of the secretaries, who worked on the broadsheet newspaper with him and she was a friend of Gloria who, at the time, was a features editor on the paper's colour supplement. Mathew had spent a week working with Gloria and by the end of the week he had managed to convince her that she should meet his old friend who, at the time, was working for another newspaper. The four of them went for a night out in Soho and after a few drinks in *The Dog and Duck* and a late night visit to *Ronnie Scott's,* it was clear that Peter and Gloria were made for each other. Although Peter was initially cross with Mathew for arranging the blind date, he would become eternally grateful to his old friend for introducing him to Gloria. They were both thirty when they met and both ready to commit to a long term relationship. Within twelve months they were living together and within two years they married, Mathew was best man at the wedding. They soon discovered that they could not have children and whilst this was a time of sadness for the two of them, it seemed to re-inforce their love for one another. Peter's parents, Stanley and Dorothy were overjoyed that Peter had settled down and truly loved Gloria. They were both in their seventies by the time Peter and Gloria married and were delighted whenever they came to visit them in Birmingham. Gloria had a personality that people found very attractive, it was the same whenever she met Mathew's family in Surrey, they would always be so happy to see her.

Peter fondly remembered Gloria reading poems at each of his parents' funerals, they had died within a few a weeks of each other and even though they were both in their eighties, it was still a shock for him. Gloria had lost her own father when she was young and instinctively knew how he was feeling, following the loss of his parents. She explained to him that, sometimes, when parents died when they are old it was more difficult for the children to come to terms with it, for the simple reason that you have known them for so long, in Peter's case more than fifty years. Gloria had never known her father as an adult and whilst his loss was terrible, her feelings at the time were that of a child.

Gloria's sudden death still felt quite unreal to Peter. She was at home in Marylebone in the kitchen and suffered a stroke. He remembered the ambulance arriving and the drive to the hospital and then, later in the evening, the doctor giving him the terrible news that she had died. He could look back now and think positively about their relationship, they had been very happy together. However, in the immediate aftermath, it had not been so easy. Mathew had driven him down to Surrey and he had spent a week there with Mathew's family. They showed him such tremendous kindness and love during such a dark time, he would never forget how much they helped him. He spent the year following Gloria's death badly depressed, drinking too much, the hangovers only made matters worse. Oddly enough, it was the investigation into the Coleville's deceit that had brought him back to life and rekindled his love of work and particularly, investigative journalism. The relationship with Isabella had been proof to himself that he had recovered, it felt completely natural and he had experienced no guilt feelings whatsoever.

As Peter crossed High Street Kensington and headed towards *The Elephant and Castle* he thought of his own very happy relationships with Gloria, his parents, Mathew and his family and then thought about the relationships which would be damaged, should the Coleville's deceit be exposed. Patricia and Simon, their daughter Emily, Julia

Norberg and her son and possibly other relations and friends, who didn't deserve the trauma that would undoubtedly be caused, were they to discover the truth. Was it really all worth it he asked himself?

Peter had this in the back of his mind as he updated Mathew on his visit to Julia Norberg's home in Bayswater. It was useful to speak with Mathew, he had a slightly more detached view of the situation and with the exception of Robert Coleville, had not met any of the leading characters involved.

"You've got to hand it to old Coleville for his sheer nerve. If what you have discovered is true, he has actually had some kind of relationship with the woman who's baby his wife abducted from the hospital, presumably, so he could keep tabs on his real son.....you couldn't make it up old boy," and Mathew continued, "all this, whilst he was a Member of Parliament as well, incredible."

"Yes, he certainly took some huge risks. My dilemma though Matt, is what to do next. On the face of it, a dreadful crime has been committed and it should be a police matter but, on the other hand, imagine the turmoil it would cause for the innocent parties." Peter replied and told Mathew of his fears, should the Coleville's deceit be exposed.

"Sounds as though we should put it to the WWSD test old boy." Suggested Mathew.

"Oh, yes," Peter smiled, "What would Sid do?"

For the best part of forty years, whenever faced with a difficult problem concerning journalistic integrity or moral responsibilities they would apply the test, named after their first editor at the Oxford Mail, Sidney Newman. Although it was a light hearted exercise, it often led to a serious discussion between the two of them, which would lead to some kind of resolution. Sidney Newman was a legendary figure in Peter's and Mathew's eyes, forthright, principled and a good decision maker, all great qualities for a newspaper editor.

"Well," Peter continued, "at some point, he would definitely contact the police and inform them of his suspicions."

"At some point?" Mathew asked.

"Yes, it would all be down to timing with Sidney I reckon," Peter suggested, "he would probably gently confront the Coleville's or, at least one of them, with the evidence before speaking with the police himself."

"In the hope that they would confess and hand themselves in?" Mathew asked.

"Yes, I think that would be Sidney's style." Peter replied and Mathew nodded in agreement.

"One for the road old boy?" Mathew got up and headed for the bar.

Margaret Coleville gazed out of the kitchen window of the farmhouse, it was a bright sunny Spring morning in Le Marche. She waved to Maurizio as he walked along the track, which ran along the side of the farmhouse. He was going hunting in the nearby forest by the look of things, for rabbit or, possibly even deer, he had one of his guns slung over his back. Maurizio waved back, she may see him later she thought. If he was successful, he would almost certainly drop by later on with a rabbit for her, which she would prepare for her supper. She watched him disappear into the distance and reflected that, like her, he was very much a morning person. He would be back in the early afternoon, have lunch, followed by a siesta. A creature of habit she thought, it wasn't always hunting of course, he had his stall at the market in Osimo to tend to once a week and he did odd jobs, carpentry, plumbing, electrical work throughout the surrounding villages and towns.

Robert was due to arrive tomorrow and Margaret had been giving his visit a lot of thought. Since the discovery that he had betrayed her and somehow, had kept in contact with their son, she had experienced an emotion that she had very rarely felt during the past forty years, anger. The guilt, coupled with the long periods of depression and anxiety she had suffered, had affected her so badly that anger was not an emotion that she was particularly familiar with. Her confidence had been so low, for so long, that fear and self-loathing were much more familiar emotions to her than anger. Of course, there were moments of anger, the car running out of petrol or, losing her wallet or even misplacing her mobile phone, she thought to herself smiling, but these were occasions when she was angry with herself. Being angry, really angry with someone else, was new. Spending more than half a lifetime being depressed and imagining that everyone else, other than herself, was happy and carefree had taken its toll. Her way of coping through this living nightmare had been to keep busy, all of the time. However mundane the task, she would throw herself into it fully until it was completed and she was exhausted or, failing that, she found something else to occupy her time. Robert was correct when he encouraged her to return to work just days after giving birth, he said it would take her mind of things and it did. Keeping constantly busy worked, to a degree. There were, of course, occasions when it was simply not possible to be busy and it was during these periods that she would rely on medication or, to be more accurate, drugs, to help her cope.

Suddenly, well at least since Simon, Patricia and Emily had returned to London, she no longer felt that she needed to be busy or, take drugs to cope. She was angry and strangely, her anger made her feel a lot better and she had become preoccupied with formulating her plans for the future. She had decided over the past twenty-four hours, since she had seen the photographs on Patricia's mobile phone that she was going to find her son, her real son. She finally had a purpose in life, an objective and a strategy was forming in her mind to achieve her objective. Oddly enough, her scientific background had become a great help, she could plan her next move dispassionately and in great detail. She would not be confronting Robert with her discovery when he arrived tomorrow. If she did, she knew only too well that he would do everything possible to prevent her seeing their son, because it would almost certainly result in their secret being discovered. This would not help her achieve her objective, so she had discounted confronting him, for now. The strategy that was forming in her mind didn't involve Robert, she knew she was on her own now.

CHAPTER TWENTY

TEHRAN - SPRING 2014

Gheytarieh Park is located in a district of the same name in north eastern Tehran. The large park was once the home of a famous Persian Qajar Dynasty minister, Amir Kabir. Taraneh Saderzadeh parked her car in a quiet side street next to the park, got out of the car and walked around to the passenger door to help her father. Mohsen Saderzadeh was now ninety years old and used a walking stick to help him whenever he ventured out of the house he shared with his daughter in Gheytarieh. Spring was always Taraneh's favourite season in Tehran, the snow melts on the Alborz mountain range and the water flows down along the street edges of the city in wide gutters, known as jubes. Her father was well known in the park and friends and acquaintances would stop and greet him asking him how he was, "Salam agha Saderzadeh, chetori?" they would call to him. Sometimes, it would take them an hour to take just a short walk because of the number of interruptions, but this was typical of Persian custom and politeness, particularly towards the elderly.

Taraneh's father had returned to Tehran in December 1978, as the revolution raged throughout Iran. Friends and family had advised him not to return from London, but he wanted to ensure that his wife and two daughters living in Tehran were safe. He was briefly imprisoned, but eventually released, on the understanding that he didn't leave the country. He never left the country again and had lived a peaceful, happy life in Gheytarieh. Taraneh also returned to Tehran following the revolution, the breakdown of her marriage a few years earlier meant she had few ties in England. Her marriage to David, a junior doctor in Oxford, had been a terrible mistake. Following the wedding in Tehran, they returned to Oxford and soon moved into a small terraced house in Jericho which, at the time, was a run-down area close to the city centre and the Radcliffe Infirmary, where she was working. It soon became apparent, at least to Taraneh, that the two of them had very different views on how they should live their lives. David's behaviour became extremely controlling, the final straw being when he insisted that Taraneh must end her career and become a full time housewife. They had been married for less than two years, when she finally walked out. Fortunately, they had no children. She moved in with her long standing friend and fellow nurse Rita in her flat in Headington, a suburb of Oxford, and continued nursing at the Radcliffe, until she returned to Iran. Whilst it was an extremely unhappy time for her, she had made a friend for life in Rita. In fact, they were still friends today and whenever Taraneh travelled to London, she would meet up with her old friend. Rita had even visited her in Tehran on one occasion and they spent a wonderful fortnight travelling around the country together. On one of Taraneh's visits to England, the two of them spent a week in Rita's hometown, Liverpool. Their backgrounds and personalities were different in virtually every respect, but they seemed to get along famously. They had both recently turned sixty and with the advent of the internet, would speak on a weekly basis using a video call.

Taraneh's father still owned the apartment in Kensington, which he had purchased when he worked at the Iranian Embassy and Taraneh would stay there on her visits to London. Her two sisters had emigrated to America in the nineteen-nineties and her mother had died three years ago, leaving just her and her father together in Tehran. In many ways, it reminded her of their days living together in

London in the nineteen-sixties and seventies. Her father was a very quiet, patient man and although he would never admit it, Taraneh had always been his favourite daughter. All those years ago he had given her the opportunity to pursue her dream and become a nurse in England and she felt it was the least she could do to look after her father in his old age. Their relationship had become one of mutual respect, she was grateful that, at such a young age, he had given her the freedom to pursue the career of her choice in London. At the time, this was quite unusual, in a society where parents are often over protective of their children. Whilst her father was naturally delighted that she was now looking after him, he was always encouraging her to travel and not to feel tied down because of him. It was for this reason, that it was not difficult for Taraneh to explain to him that she needed to return to London in a few weeks' time. There were some issues concerning the lease on the freehold of the apartment in Kensington that needed her attention.

"Of course you must go Taraneh dear, I will be fine here you know that." He told her.

They were walking slowly, arm in arm, through the park.

"I will arrange for Maryam Khanum to come in each day when I am away father, I have already spoken with her and just need to tell her the exact dates when I will be away." Taranheh explained.

"I am not completely helpless you know Taraneh dear." her father laughed, "but I appreciate your concern and Maryam Khanum cooks a very good chelo kebab you know!"

"Better than mine?" Taraneh teased him.

The two of them discussed the merits of good Persian cooking as they quietly continued their stroll through the beautiful Gheytarieh Park.

153

CHAPTER TWENTY-ONE

ROBERT'S DIARIES

Robert and Margaret returned to London together following their week at the farmhouse in Le Marche. Margaret had spent the week in Italy secretly planning how to discover her real son's whereabouts and had decided upon a course of action. For the first time since she had returned from the maternity hospital all those years ago, she felt a sense of purpose in life and it was the thought of seeing her son, along with her anger towards Robert, which was driving her forward. She had been betrayed, there was no doubt about that, but rather than letting the anger consume her, she had channeled it, into what she now thought of as a crusade. Since discovering Robert's deceit, she now saw, in her own mind, the future as a simple battle between right and wrong. She had been wronged and felt that her husband's treacherous behaviour had wiped the slate clean of the guilt she had experienced ever since she had abducted another mother's child. The guilt she had experienced for more than forty years had evaporated, almost overnight. Whilst in Italy, she would wake, sometimes in the early hours of the morning and go over the plans she had been making, time and time again, until she dropped off to sleep again. She found the experience enjoyable and was counting the days until she returned to London, when she could get down to the real business of finding her son and when the time was right, punishing Robert for his treachery.

Robert used the week in Italy preparing for a busy week ahead when he returned to London. His memoirs were to be published that week and along with his agent, he would be embarking on a week-long, quite low-key, book promotional tour of the UK, involving book signing, local radio interviews, although he did have one arranged on BBC Radio Four's Book Club, as well as a couple of appearances at book fairs, where he would answer questions from the audience. Following the tour, Robert had booked flights to Venice and a luxury hotel, as a treat for himself and Margaret. They would spend a few days there, before driving south to the farmhouse, where they would spend another week together.

Back in Chelsea on the Sunday evening, Margaret helped Robert pack for his tour of the UK and at eight o'clock the following morning his agent picked him up and they drove off for their first engagement in Oxford. When he had left, Margaret lost no time at all and headed straight to Robert's study, where she weighed up the task before her. Robert's diaries, all fifty leather bound years of them, sat on the shelves before her. It was a daunting sight but, she knew that if she was to discover the whereabouts of her son and the woman who had brought him up, she had to examine them in detail. In scientific terms, which was the way in which she was approaching the task, she would undertake a forensic examination. Margaret was interested in the years 1973-2013, forty years of diaries. She knew, from discussions she had with Robert when he was planning to write his memoirs, that the diaries were generally divided into two parts, his political life and his personal life. Each diary held one full page for each day of the year and she had already estimated that she may have to read through the best part of fifteen thousand pages and only had six days to complete the exercise. Hopefully, she thought, she would find the evidence she was looking for well before she read through all of the diaries. Whilst it was, indeed, a daunting task, Margaret felt a thrill of anticipation at the task ahead and was determined to undertake a thorough forensic search to find the evidence of Robert's relationship with the young blonde woman in the photographs. Inevitably, this would lead her to her own son, she was convinced of it. She had decided upon an extremely detailed approach to the search and was keen to discover trends, perhaps being revealed over a number of years.

The first few days were the hardest, getting used to Robert's handwriting and style of writing was difficult enough in itself. Throughout the nineteen seventies and eighties, the diaries were dominated by his political life and on some days his personal life only merited one or two sentences. *By the time I returned home from the Commons, M&S (Margaret and Simon) were fast asleep* was a common entry. Another difficult aspect when reading through the diaries was the continual use of acronyms for organisations, as well as the use of initials and even nicknames for certain individuals. It took Margaret three days to read through the nineteen-seventies and eighties and she had found nothing of any substance. At times, she struggled to focus on what she was actually searching for and the fact that she was only sleeping between four and five hours each night and barely eating, wasn't helping matters.

The breakthrough came late in the evening of the fourth day. By the mid nineteen-nineties, Margaret had started travelling more and more to the, newly bought, farmhouse in Italy, which she had thrown herself into updating and refurbishing. It was a huge project, as she liked to call it and she would shuttle between London and Le Marche several times a year. She noticed that her trips to Italy were reflected in the diaries, *M to Italy for two weeks* was a common entry around this time. Margaret wasn't exactly sure why, but she noticed that by the time she had started reading through the 1997 diary, more often than not, her trips to Italy coincided with Robert meeting his accountant. According to the diary, she had made six trips to Italy in 1997 and Robert had arranged a meeting with his accountant on five separate occasions coinciding with her trips. The trend continued throughout 1998 and 1999 and Margaret spent most of the night looking through the later diaries, right up to the current year. She knew what she was looking for now and the searches for her trips to Italy alone or, occasionally with Simon and later with Patricia were easy to find, because she had kept her own old personal pocket diaries, filo faxes and online diaries and could quickly cross-reference the dates of the trips to Italy in her diaries, against the dates in Robert's diaries. Sure enough, during nearly all of her trips to Italy without Robert, he had met his accountant, sometimes on more than one occasion.

It was nearly four o'clock in the morning when Margaret found records of Robert's accounts, they were neatly filed, year by year. She noted that up until 1997 they had been prepared by Roland Williamson. She vaguely remembered meeting Roland and his wife at some function or other back in the nineteen-eighties. She returned to Robert's diaries and saw that at the same time each year when the accounts were prepared up until 1997, there was an entry which said, *meeting with RW accountant*. By the time Margaret started to look at the records of Robert's accounts from 1997 to 2012, she had a very good idea of what she was going to find. Robert's accounts for that period had been prepared by Julia Norberg Accountancy Limited, with a registered address in Bayswater and he had been meeting his accountant on a regular basis, whenever she was away at the farmhouse in Italy. Margaret sat back in the leather chair in Robert's office and found that her hands were trembling but, at the same time she felt strangely exhilarated. She was genuinely shocked that, after all she had gone through to keep their secret, the lies she had told over the years, the damage to her mental health and wellbeing, Robert had betrayed her in the most hurtful way imaginable, it was hard to believe. She was now almost certain that all of the evidence she had found over the years of Robert's affairs with other women had been deliberately fabricated to provide a false trail, a smokescreen, to hide the affair that had gone on for more than forty years. An affair with Simon's real mother, the woman who had brought up their own son, Julia Norberg.

Erik Norberg's flight landed on time at Heathrow Airport. He had emailed Julia the previous day to tell her that, unexpectedly, the bank had recalled him from New York. The London office was in crisis, following the surprise resignation of the bank's chief executive and the chairman had personally asked Erik to return to London to help steady the ship, as he put it during a late night telephone call. Erik saw it as further evidence that his career was in the ascendency and it actually crossed his mind that he might even be offered the chief executive role. His apartment in fashionable Shoreditch was let for another three months, so he would be staying with Julia, for the time being. However, before going to Bayswater, he was met by a driver at the airport and driven straight to the City for an extraordinary board meeting, which had been called by the chairman.

In Bayswater, Julia was preparing Erik's room ahead of his arrival. She was pleasantly surprised when she read Erik's email the previous day and delighted that he would be staying with her for the near future. She had spoken with Robert earlier, who was on tour promoting his book, to let him know that Erik would be staying with her for a while. What she really meant, but didn't say, was that Robert would not be able to visit her in Bayswater whilst Erik was staying with her. It was an unspoken agreement they had always kept, at least since Erik grew up, that when he was staying with Julia, Robert would not visit her. During their telephone conversation, Julia detected that Robert was not himself. He sounded anxious about something, which was very unlike him. When she asked him whether everything was alright, he was quite short with her and said he had a dinner engagement and had to go. In her excitement at the thought of Erik coming to stay, Julia soon forgot about Robert's sharpness on the phone.

CHAPTER TWENTY-TWO

THE BOOK SIGNING

Whilst Margaret had started her trawl through her husband's diaries, he had checked into the *Old Parsonage*, a smart hotel near Oxford's city centre. The reviews of his, recently published, memoirs in the Sunday papers had been favourable and it had given him a bit of a lift, before his week-long promotional tour. His first engagement was an interview on BBC Radio Oxford, followed by a book signing appointment at *Blackwell's Bookshop* in Broad Street. The radio interview went well, most of the questions concerned his relationship with the three different Prime Ministers that he had served under during his time as an MP and a Minister. He was pleasantly surprised that he was asked about his family's humble beginnings and specifically, his parents' life working in the rag trade in East London. Robert had written about their life in the book and when asked about them, was conscious that it was the first time that he had ever spoken about his parents in public, which now seemed strange to him, bearing in mind how proud of them he had always been. Consequently, he arrived at *Blackwell's* feeling positive about the rest of the week. There was plenty of signage, advertising the book signing outside the bookshop and the interviewer at BBC Radio Oxford, had also mentioned to his listeners that Robert would be signing books there from three o'clock.

Peter Wilson got off the train at Oxford station and headed, on foot, towards the city centre. He had been sent the itinerary of Robert Coleville's promotional tour by email, from his agent presumably he thought, because he was on a list of those people who had helped with the book. As he walked along Beaumont Street, past the *Ashmolean Museum*, Peter thought how little Oxford ever changes, certainly in the centre of the city. He wondered whether Temple Cowley, the suburb where he had digs in the early nineteen-seventies, had changed much. In those days, virtually everyone living in Cowley had someone in their family working at the car factory. At that time, more than twenty thousand people were employed at the *Morris Motors* and *Pressed Steel Fisher* factories and Peter could remember the surrounding roads being blocked by cyclists when shifts ended. Recently, he had read about the success of the *BMW* factory on the same site, which now produced the *Mini*, but was aware that it only employed about a quarter of the number of people who worked there forty years ago and wondered how that had affected the area.

He turned left into St Giles and on the spur of the moment he decided to have a look at the Radcliffe Infirmary building from the Woodstock Road. He had read a while ago that it was no longer a hospital and was now used by the University of Oxford. He stood outside looking at the building, the façade remained unchanged, listed he assumed and the small chapel next to the old building was also unaltered. Peter's mind wandered and he thought about Taraneh Saderzadeh and how strange it was that the story, which she had told him all those years ago whilst he was recovering from his injuries in this beautiful old building, had brought him back to Oxford today. He wondered what had become of her, he remembered her telling him that she was to marry a doctor and that was the last time he had seen or heard from her. Shortly afterwards he had moved to London and started a new life.

Peter was still thinking about Taraneh and his days working at the Oxford Mail when he entered *Blackwell's* bookshop on Broad Street. He noted from the signage that the book signing was taking place on the first floor and

161

climbed the stairs of the beautiful old bookshop. Sir Robert Coleville was sat behind a large desk in one of the alcoves. A pile of books sat on the table in front of him and a queue of about half a dozen people were waiting to have their copies of his memoirs signed. Peter joined the queue and spotted Robert's agent talking to one of the staff, he remembered him from the dinner party in Hampstead. Robert didn't notice Peter until he was next in line. He looked up and smiled.

"I had a feeling you might turn up sooner or later." Robert said calmly.

"Hello Bob," Peter replied, "you know why I'm here then?"

Robert was suddenly aware that his agent and one or two of the customers were now listening.

"Yes of course I do Peter, to get your copy of my book signed!" Robert laughed. "The least I can do after all the help you have given me. I've booked a table at *Gee's* on the Banbury Road for six o'clock, will you join me?"

Robert handed Peter the signed copy of the memoirs and beckoned the next customer in the queue.

"Thank you Bob, I'll see you there." Peter replied and acknowledged Robert's agent with a nod as he left.

Peter had a quick look around the magnificent Norrington Room in the basement of the bookshop, before heading for the *Turf Tavern*. He had a couple of hours to spare before dinner and he fancied a pint.

Erik arrived at his mother's apartment in Bayswater, following the extraordinary board meeting in the City. Julia had prepared his favourite meal, a risotto with fresh asparagus, to welcome him back home. Over dinner, they caught up on each other's news.

"How did the board meeting go?" Julia asked, whilst refilling their glasses with white wine.

162

"Oh, it was fine mum, there's a minor crisis and the chairman has asked me to stay in London for a few weeks to steady the ship, since the banking crisis they seem to panic over anything!" Erik replied.

Julia smiled, she was always secretly pleased that Erik still called her mum, even though he had now turned forty and was a senior executive at the bank.

"What about you mum, the business is doing well?" Erik asked.

Julia remembered how modest her son had always been, playing down his own successes and cleverly changing the subject to ask others how life was treating them.

"Fine thank you, I recently took on a new client, nice guy, a journalist called Peter Wilson, quite well known in his day, won lots of awards. Have you heard of him?" Julia asked.

"Yes, I have actually, although it was before my time, we went to the same college at Oxford. When I was there, his name occasionally cropped up, only because he was an old boy and had become a successful journalist I suppose." Erik replied.

They enjoyed a fresh fruit salad for dessert and finished off the bottle of wine, Julia noticed that Erik had drank more than usual, he normally would only have one glass with dinner. She brought some coffee on a tray from the kitchen and as she sat down she thought she could detect a little bit of tension in the air when Erik spoke.

"There's something I really need to tell you about mum." Erik said deliberately avoiding eye contact with Julia. She noticed that Erik was nervous, which was totally out of character.

"Don't tell me you're getting married!" Julia blurted out, in an attempt to lighten the atmosphere.

"I wish you hadn't said that mum, it makes this even more difficult for me". Erik said looking at the ceiling.

Julia stopped smiling, it suddenly dawned on her that this was a serious moment.

"I'm sorry Erik that was silly of me, what is it you want to tell me?" she asked quietly.

"There's no easy way of saying this, so here goes, I'm gay mum." Erik felt himself blush as he waited for Julia's reaction.

Julia looked at her son with a pleasant, gentle smile. This hadn't come as a complete surprise to her, she had thought about the likelihood that Erik might be gay from time to time, but to hear him actually tell her, was still a bit of a shock and she wasn't quite sure what to say.

"Well, are you disappointed in me mum?" Erik asked, more confident now.

"I'm disappointed that it's taken you until you're forty-one years old to tell me." Julia got up, walked around the table and took Erik in her arms.

"Do your friends know and what about the bank?" Julia asked.

"Yes, my friends know and most people at the bank know, but it's not something that I advertise! Anyway, employers have to be very careful not to discriminate these days and it certainly hasn't held me back in my career."

"Well, as far as I'm concerned Erik, I love you as much now as I did when we sat down to dinner, if that helps at all."

"Thanks mum, it does help, it's a weight off my shoulders I can tell you. Can I just ask one small favour though, can we not talk about it a lot, it's just who I am, if you see what I mean." Erik said.

"Of course, and thank you for telling me." Julia smiled.

Gee's restaurant was quiet when Peter arrived. Only three tables were occupied in the beautiful glass conservatory. At one of them, in the far right hand corner near to the Banbury Road, he spotted Robert Coleville. He stood up as Peter approached the table and shook hands.

"Thank you for inviting me Bob, the book signing looked as though it was going well." Peter said.

"Yes, I wasn't quite sure what to expect or even if anyone would turn up at all, but I was pleasantly surprised with the numbers. Shall we order some food and wine before we talk Peter, I don't know about you but I'm starving!" Robert said, passing Peter a menu.

Peter remembered when he heard Robert speak that he couldn't help liking him, even though he felt very angry at the way he had behaved. Whenever their paths had crossed over the years, Robert had always come across as being genuinely friendly, which was not always the case with politicians. Peter could suddenly hear Sidney Newman advising him all those years ago that, just because a person does something very bad in their life, it doesn't mean they are completely wicked. They ordered quickly and ate the main course in near silence. When the plates had been cleared away, Robert folded his napkin and refilled their glasses with the red wine he had ordered.

"I'll tell you what Peter, why don't you tell me everything you know and then I'll fill in any gaps?" Robert suggested.

Peter realised from Robert's suggestion that he was aware that his secret had been uncovered and he quickly decided that he would only tell him the really important facts that he had unearthed and then see what he had to say for himself.

"It's straightforward really Bob, I know that Julia Norberg brought up your real son and that you and Margaret brought up her son, Simon." Peter paused and had a drink of wine. "Which, in itself, is none of my business. However, inadvertently, I discovered that a serious crime was committed over forty years ago, when you and Margaret deliberately abducted Julia Norberg's baby from the maternity hospital." Peter wasn't really sure whether or not Robert was involved with the crime at the time it was committed, but he thought that accusing him would give him the opportunity to explain exactly what happened.

Robert was speechless for a few seconds, it was the first time that he had ever heard anyone, other than Margaret, speak about the dreadful secret that they had shared for more than half of their lives and hearing someone else talk openly about the enormity of what they had done, suddenly shocked him. It crossed his mind that, after so long, the secret had become normal to him, this was new and different. He sat quietly for a few moments and composed himself.

"Margaret told me that she saw you looking at the photograph that evening when you came for dinner and how you reacted with surprise when you saw the one with the nanny holding Simon. Taraneh Saderzadeh, that was her name, we shortened it to Tara. I remember the surname, because I knew her father who was a diplomat at the Iranian Embassy at the time and told me his daughter was looking for a job. Oddly enough," Robert smiled, "he's mentioned in my book, he helped us sign an important defence contract. You knew her then Peter, when she went to work as a nurse in Oxford I suppose?"

"Sounds as though you've been doing some detective work yourself Bob!" Peter replied.

"Finding out that you started career in Oxford wasn't difficult Peter, it took me five minutes on the computer to confirm that."

"Even so, it's a big assumption for you to make that Taraneh told me about her suspicions." Peter suggested.

"You weren't the only person she confided in Peter, she told our housekeeper at the time that she was concerned. Beryl's still alive you know, in her nineties, I paid her a visit recently to check whether Tara had spoken with her at the time, she told me that she had."

166

Robert topped up their glasses with the last of the wine and called the waiter over to order some coffee.

"Julia told me you've been to see her in Bayswater," Robert continued, "Another new client was how she described you. I'm not sure how Julia will take all of this when she finds out the truth." Robert's voice faltered at this point.

"She has no idea?" Peter asked.

"None....when I met Julia it was shortly after Simon and Erik were born, she gave him a Scandinavian name. I found out she was working at the library, a stone's throw from our house in Hampstead and I deliberately befriended her so that I could keep tabs on my son. I'm ashamed of myself for doing that, it was despicable, wicked. Margaret had no idea what I was doing and she hasn't to this day, as far as I know. Julia was struggling to make ends meet, her background in Sweden was tragic and I suddenly found myself genuinely wanting to help this young, single mother and Erik of course. Erik still has no idea I'm his real father you know."

"That was quite a risk you took as a young MP." Peter said.

"After what Margaret had done, it didn't seem such a big risk at the time. In fact, to be perfectly honest, nothing that has happened in my life since that terrible day when Margaret abducted the baby has felt particularly risky. What changed everything, is that I fell in love with Julia. It knocked me for six to be honest, I just hadn't expected that to happen. I told her from the very beginning that I was married with a young son and an MP and had no intention of leaving my wife and eventually, she told me that she loved me as well and was prepared to put up with that. Remarkable really. I've often wondered why she agreed to this strange life she has led, a lot to do with the way she was treated as she grew up I would imagine. That and her overriding objective to give Erik the best upbringing she could. I used to try and help her financially you know, but she wouldn't hear of it, so I helped her and Erik in other ways, behind the scenes, I helped get her a job in the Commons and Erik his job at the bank. You know he's on the verge of becoming the chief executive!" Robert smiled warmly. "Will you have a cognac with me Peter, I could certainly do with one?"

Peter nodded and when the waiter arrived with the drinks, Robert continued.

"This is not in any way an excuse for Margaret's behaviour or, for my reaction to it, but Margaret was ill when she brought Julia's child home. She'd miscarried and following that she had a still born baby and it affected her mental health. When she was told that Simon, her newborn baby was slightly jaundiced, she panicked. Years later, she told me that she'd heard voices in her head urging her on to switch the babies around in the incubators. Even so, it's unforgivable, lots of parents have problems, but they don't respond by abducting a child. She told me what she had done as soon as she arrived home with Simon. Looking back, I think I went into shock. I remember driving to my parents' graves in Golder's Green to ask them for advice."

"Really?" Peter interrupted, "Did they give you any....advice I mean?"

"No, of course not, I just didn't know what to do. Anyway, my father would have told me to go to the police immediately. He was the most law abiding man I've ever known. I'd pulled myself together by the time I got home. I sat Margaret down, she was in a right state, and told her that we had a secret that we would share for the rest of our lives. We made an agreement, a pact if you like, that we would never breathe a word about it to anyone, ever. Well, I've broken that agreement for the first time today." Robert stopped talking and looked up from the table at Peter. "You're the first person, other than Margaret, that I've

168

spoken with about this in more than forty years. It's a long time to keep a secret Peter."

Peter looked at Robert and thought to himself again that he couldn't help liking him, even though he knew his behaviour had been appalling and the fallout from all of this could be devastating for everyone concerned.

"I always said you were a good journalist Peter." Robert laughed, "So what happens next, I can't see you selling your story to the tabloids, not your style."

"No, I wouldn't do that, it's really up to you to decide what happens next Bob, but now that I know the truth, I can't ignore it, either you and Margaret go to the police when you're ready or, if you don't, I will."

"Thank you Peter, that's very good of you, we're going to Italy next week, when this book tour has finished, it was meant to be a treat, a short break in Venice and then a few days at the farmhouse. I'll speak to Margaret then, you have my word, it won't be easy, she's had her suspicions about you, but she knows nothing about Julia and Erik."

It was Friday evening and Margaret was expecting Robert back from his promotional book tour the following morning. They would fly to Venice on Sunday, where they would stay for two nights at a luxury hotel near to St Mark's Square, before hiring a car and driving down to the farmhouse in Le Marche.

Since finding evidence of Robert's betrayal, Margaret had felt energised and even empowered, feelings she hadn't experienced for many years. She felt totally in control of her life and it was as if her discovery, somehow excused her from the abduction of Julia Norberg's child from the maternity home. She had been making detailed plans for their trip to Italy and her own return and she was feeling pleased with herself. She smiled to herself, thinking that under different circumstances, Robert would have been very impressed with her for showing such imagination and

169

attention to detail with the plans she had made. To reward herself, she poured a large gin and tonic. She'd barely drank at all for the past forty years, partly because of all the medication she had been taking, but now she found that she was enjoying alcohol again and the warm feeling it gave her. She decided to send Robert a text message before she went to bed.

'*Have a safe journey home darling, looking forward to our trip to Italy together, nite nite, love M*'

CHAPTER TWENTY-THREE

REVENGE

Peter and Mathew were enjoying a late lunch in *The Elephant and Castle* and Peter was telling his old friend about his dinner in Oxford with Robert Coleville.

"And do you think he'll actually tell Margaret to go to the police?" Mathew asked, slightly cynically.

"Yes, I think he probably will, I made it clear that if he doesn't, I will go to the police, but God only knows how she'll react when he tells her, that will almost certainly depend on how much he's prepared to say and possibly upon how much she already knows." Peter replied.

"How much she already knows?" Mathew asked quizzically.

"Yes, well we know that Robert has had an affair lasting more than forty years with Julia Norberg and he believes that Margaret knows nothing about it, but can you believe that? I'm not sure I do Matt." Peter said.

"But if Margaret does go to the police and turns herself in, presumably there will be an investigation, Julia will be traced and there's a very good chance that will lead to her affair with Robert being disclosed anyway." Mathew suggested.

"Possibly, whatever happens though, I don't think we've heard the end of this story yet and talking about the end of stories, I went for diner with Isabella last night and she told me she's going to Spain."

"What, on holiday old boy?" Mathew asked.

"No, to live unfortunately, another Spanish television company has offered her a job in Madrid, which is too good to turn down I'm afraid Matt." Peter replied.

"Sorry to hear that Peter." Mathew said, with a slightly concerned look on his face.

"Me too, but you don't need to worry about me Matt, Isabella was good for me and she helped me get over my grieving for Gloria." Peter smiled, "So, I'm footloose and fancy free again, shall we have another pint?"

Margaret was looking out of the farmhouse window, from which she could clearly see Maurizio's white van parked on his drive. It was seven o'clock in the morning and the next few minutes would be critical to the success of her plans, not just for today she thought, but for the rest of her life.

Venice had been wonderful, although at times she did feel that Robert had been preoccupied, as if something was on his mind, which was unusual for him. Conversely, she had felt surprisingly relaxed, particularly bearing in mind the plan she was about to execute. Robert had actually commented on her relaxed mood and once or twice, she caught him looking at her with a slightly puzzled expression on his face. However, she was enjoying this new experience of feeling confident and was sure that she had behaved normally enough in Venice and that Robert had not suspected anything untoward.

They had hired a car there on the Wednesday morning and had decided to break their journey on the autostrada to Le Marche by stopping the night in Ravenna. Neither of them had visited the city before and they were both keen to see the colourful mosaics on many of the buildings in its centre. Whilst in Venice, Margaret had been reading about the city and noted that the celebrated Italian poet Dante had died and was buried in Ravenna. It crossed her mind that she had spent forty years travelling through hell, much like

172

Dante's journey in his great work the Inferno. An appropriate place to stop on their way to Le Marche, she had thought to herself.

It was early Thursday evening when they finally arrived at the farmhouse and they were both tired, they had shared the driving but the journey had demanded maximum concentration on the busy autostrada. They were in bed by ten o'clock and Margaret rose at six a.m. leaving Robert fast asleep. It was not unusual for Margaret to get up early, she had always been an early riser.

It was seven-fifteen when Maurizio appeared and unlocked the back doors of his white van. It took him less than half an hour to load his goods into the back of the van. It was market day in nearby Osimo and Maurizio would have his stall setup there by nine o'clock. Margaret breathed a sigh of relief as she watched him drive off, he would have a busy day ahead of him, the weather was good and the market would be crowded. When she could no longer see the van from the kitchen window, Margaret slipped on her shoes and calmly walked around to Maurizio's house next door. She was pleased to see that he had hidden the spare key in the usual place. Margaret went inside, immediately found what she was looking for and was back in the farmhouse within minutes.

Robert woke at nine o'clock and they had breakfast together in the kitchen, Maurizio had been in the day before and kindly left them some Italian brioche and jam. Margaret had decided to confront Robert immediately after breakfast, her timescales were tight because the flight back to London Stansted would leave Ancona at mid-day and the drive to the airport would take her the best part of an hour. So far, her plans were running smoothly, but were about to be rudely interrupted. Robert had been unusually quiet during breakfast and Margaret noticed that his hand was trembling slightly as he poured them both another cup of coffee.

"Peter Wilson came to see me whilst I was in Oxford." He suddenly announced.

"The journalist?" For a moment, Margaret was thrown by Robert's announcement and she couldn't quite place Peter Wilson.

"Yes, the guy who came to dinner that night in Hampstead, you were suspicious of him when you caught him looking at the photos on the credenza, remember?" Robert asked irritably.

Margaret hadn't expected this and could feel her herself shaking.

"Yes of course I remember, what did he want?" she stammered.

"He wants us to go to the police and tell them that you brought someone else's baby home from the hospital." Robert told her.

Margaret noticed that Robert had said 'someone else's baby' and this suddenly made her extremely angry, he knew exactly whose baby they had returned home from the hospital with that terrible day.

"He has discovered our secret Margaret." Robert continued, "He knows that Simon is not our son."

"How does he know?" Margaret's voice was raised and it surprised Robert.

"The photograph." Robert replied quietly.

Margaret looked puzzled, "The photograph?"

"He recognised the nanny in the photo, Taraneh Saderzadeh, they met when he was a young reporter in Oxford and she went there to take up nursing. She told him that she suspected that Simon was not our son." Robert said calmly.

Margaret had momentarily forgotten her own plans and was trying to understand what her husband was telling her.

"Why did she suspect us?" she asked.

174

"Apparently, she heard us arguing about it late one night after a party we had thrown. She told Beryl about her suspicions as well." Robert told her.

"How do you know that?" Margaret asked.

"I went to see her in the nursing home and she told me." Margaret stood up from the kitchen table and looked across at Robert.

"Is there anything else you want to tell me?" she asked.

"I think that's enough for one day, don't you?" he replied angrily.

"No I don't Robert," and there was something in the way that she said it that made him feel very nervous. Margaret was shouting now as she turned and left the kitchen, "you see, there is something that you have hidden from me for more than forty years, you have betrayed me and you are both going to pay for that!"

Robert stood up and watched incredulously as she returned to the kitchen a few seconds later holding a shotgun, which was pointing at him. She left no time for him to speak, she just pulled the trigger. The noise was deafening and surprised her, much louder in the confined space of a farmhouse kitchen, than when Maurizio had taught her to shoot rabbits in the forest. Firing the shotgun had nearly resulted in Margaret losing her balance and when she had recovered she looked at Robert, who was now laying on the stone floor with blood dripping from what looked like a head wound. Margaret suddenly remembered her plan. She calmly took the shotgun and returned it next door to Maurizio's gun cabinet. She hurried back to the farmhouse and went upstairs, she had deliberately not unpacked when they had returned from Venice the previous afternoon and her small case, which she could carry on the flight as hand luggage, was sat waiting for her in the wardrobe, along with her passport and flight ticket.

The journey to the airport went very smoothly and easily took less than an hour and on arrival, she was relieved to see that her flight was on time. She would be back in central London by mid-afternoon, perfect timing to carry out the next stage of her plan.

Julia and Erik had spent the morning at her home in Bayswater. Erik was working from home for the day, preparing a presentation he would be giving to the bank's board of directors the following morning. Even during the short time since Erik had told Julia about his sexuality their relationship had changed. They could both tell that it had changed and were now happy to sit and talk, revealing experiences in their lives that they had never shared before. Julia, particularly, seemed to feel comfortable telling Erik more about her early life in London. Of course, Erik had asked about his father before and Julia had always answered him honestly, telling him that the relationship had been a foolish one night stand and she had never seen his father again. However, she now felt able to put some context around the events that led to her pregnancy, being abandoned as a child by an alcoholic mother who had suffered from mental illness, which ultimately led to her being adopted and the premature death of her adoptive mother from a brain hemorrhage when she was just sixteen. All this trauma had ultimately resulted in her being alone in London with little money, whilst expecting a child.

Erik had always been proud of his mother and his admiration for her had only increased as she told him more about her early life. As a young child, he had vague memories of their life together in Hampstead. He could remember the trips to the seaside, being picked up by Julia from his infants' school and his first day at boarding school. Erik had often wondered about the kind, tall, handsome man who had been present during those early years and what had become of him. He particularly remembered one day at the seaside just before he went off to boarding school, he must have been seven or eight he supposed. It was a glorious warm day and he was lying on the beach reading a comic. Julia and her friend, who she referred to as Uncle Robert when he was present, were sat on the seafront with their feet in the water. He could distinctly remember then sharing a kiss and afterwards Julia turned around looking nervously towards where he was sat on the beach. It was an unusual show of affection between the two of them in his company and he quickly turned the page of his comic pretending he hadn't seen them. By the time he had left boarding school and gone to university, he no longer saw his mother's mysterious friend, Uncle Robert, but he often had a strange feeling that he was still present, somewhere in the background. He had never asked Julia about him and he wasn't going to ask now, but he had an idea that she was building up the courage to tell him about the relationship herself.

It took nearly three hours for Robert to regain conciousness and open his eyes. He was lying on his side on the hard stone of the farmhouse kitchen floor and was looking under the kitchen table across to the door. It took a few moments for him to understand why he was lying there. His head was throbbing and when he touched his forehead, he could feel sticky congealed blood. He tried to lift himself up but couldn't move his left leg, it felt numb. He lay still for a while trying to piece together exactly what had happened. After Margaret had fired the shotgun at him, he remembered staggering and hitting his head on what must have been the kitchen table as he fell. The shotgun shell must have hit him in the leg, he thought. He remembered lying in agony for several minutes and was sure that he heard Margaret leaving the kitchen and a few minutes later the car engine starting, he must have passed out after that. Suddenly, he recalled the last thing that Margaret had said before she shot him and it made him shiver, "you are both going to pay," she had told him. It was the word 'both' that made him realise that he had to act quickly, he had to do something to stop her because he was sure that she was on her way, heading back to London, Bayswater to be exact, having left him for dead.

Robert felt inside the breast pocket of his shirt, where he normally kept his mobile phone but it wasn't there. Christ, he thought to himself, perhaps I left it in the bedroom. Slowly lifting his head up off the floor, he managed to turn so he could look across, in the opposite direction, towards the kitchen sink. His spirits lifted slightly when he spotted his phone, it had become lodged to one side of the pedal bin, it must have dropped out of his pocket when he fell, he thought. He knew that his one chance was to try and crawl across the kitchen floor and reach it. He desperately tried to think whether he had charged it up overnight, but couldn't remember. He lay still for a few moments trying to work out how best to move across the kitchen floor, his left leg wouldn't move and seemed to be completely without feeling and his head ached to high heaven. He wondered what time it was, he knew it was about nine-thirty when they had breakfast, his watch would be next to his bedside table he thought. How long had he been lying there he wondered and thought to himself that he was glad it was summer in Italy or he would have frozen to death on the cold stone floor. He was actually cross with himself for a few moments, for not having worn the shirt with the button on the breast pocket, his phone would still be there if he had and not on the other side of the bloody kitchen! Still feeling terribly weak, he started to use just his arms to pull himself across the floor towards the phone, cursing to himself that it was such a big kitchen and they should have bought that lovely little apartment they had been to see in Genoa all those years ago! It took the best part of half an hour before he managed to stretch out an arm and grab hold of his phone. He was absolutely exhausted, but relieved to see that it was almost fully charged. It was four o'clock in the afternoon in

Italy, three o'clock in England. He thought to himself that Margaret would be back in London, he knew the times of the flights from Ancona like the back of his hand, they'd taken so many of them over the years. Whilst he had been edging himself across the kitchen floor, he had worked out a course of action to try and stop Margaret. Robert paged through his contact list and rang Peter Wilson's number. The call immediately went to voicemail. Robert sighed and left a message telling Peter that this was an emergency and he must ring him back as soon as possible. He decided to himself that he would give Peter fifteen minutes before trying something else, although he wasn't sure what! He needn't have worried, within five minutes his phone rang.

"Peter, is that you?"

"Yes, are you alright Bob, what's happened, I thought you were in Italy with Margaret?" Peter asked.

Strangely, considering the circumstances, Robert smiled at being called Bob by Peter with that broad Brummie accent.

"Listen Peter and please don't ask too many questions, are you in London?"

"Yes, I was on the tube when you rang." Peter told him.

"You must go to Bayswater now, immediately, I think Margaret is on her way there and is going to harm Julia!"

"OK, I can do that." Peter replied calmly.

Christ, he's a cool character, Robert thought.

"I'll ring Frank, the porter in Julia's block and tell him to give you a spare key to the flat when you arrive." Robert said.

"And you Bob, are you alright?" Peter asked.

"Yes, I'm fine," Robert lied, "please just go there now and call me when you find Julia and let me know that she is safe, please Peter!"

Robert ended the call and lay on the kitchen floor feeling utterly exhausted.

179

Margaret had deliberately left the car in the short stay car park at Stansted, to enable her to make a quick exit from the airport. When they had parked it there, Robert had questioned why she hadn't used the much cheaper mid-stay parking and she had lied to him that there was a special offer for the short stay parking, so there was very little difference in the price. She smiled to herself at the thought of this, as she drove out of the car park. It was mid-afternoon and if she put her foot down, she would be in Bayswater before the rush hour started in earnest. Margaret didn't feel at all tired, even though she had already experienced a tumultuous day, in fact, she felt alert and was looking forward to executing the final stage of her plan. She had always been a very good driver, much better than Robert she thought to herself, although she never mentioned it to him. The journey took just over an hour. She had pre-booked the car park on the Bayswater Road, just to be on the safe side and drove straight into her pre-designated slot. Margaret opened the boot of the car and retrieved the carving knife, which she had hidden before she left for Italy, in the compartment which held the spare tyre. She slipped the knife into her shoulder bag and covered it with her scarf.

Arriving at the apartment block, she smiled at the elderly porter and headed for the lift. Julia Norberg was a little surprised when her doorbell rang, she hadn't been expecting anyone and unexpected visitors normally used the intercom system or, asked Frank, the porter, to call her. Looking through the front door spyhole, she saw a tall elegant lady waiting patiently for her to open door. She looked vaguely familiar, but Julia couldn't place her.

"Good afternoon, I'm Margaret Coleville, Robert's wife, you must be Julia?" the elegant lady asked with a smile.

"Er…yes, yes you'd better come in." Julia answered, her mind racing.

Margaret followed Julia through to the lounge.

"Can I get you anything, would you like to sit down?" Julia asked, struggling to concentrate. Over the years, she had occasionally thought about this moment happening and wondered what she would do under these circumstances. Now that it was actually happening, her brain had seemed to stop working properly and she could feel her heart pounding.

"No thank you, I'd rather stand, this shouldn't take long, I expect you know why I am here Robert has told me everything!" Margaret said.

Julia looked at her closely and realised that she was lying, Robert would never have told her everything. This seemed to give her confidence and she suddenly felt quite angry, who does this woman think she is coming into my home, she thought to herself.

"Oh, really, so what has he told you?" Julia asked challengingly.

"That you've both betrayed me and have hidden my child from me for forty years!" Margaret's voice was raised by now and she was visibly shaking, "but I don't care about your sordid little affair, I just want to see my son, where is he?" she shouted.

Julia was confused and beginning to feel frightened, what was this woman taking about, demanding to see her son.

Suddenly, everything seemed to happen very quickly, Julia could still hear Margaret shouting that she had already dealt with Robert, when Peter Wilson, accompanied by another man who she didn't recognise, burst through the front door, along the hallway and into the lounge. Julia looked at Peter and thought to herself, what on earth is he doing here and how did he get in? She was staring at him, expecting some kind of explanation but she noticed that neither Peter, nor the other man, were paying her any attention, they were both staring at Margaret, who was now holding, what looked like, a brand new stainless steel carving knife in her right hand. Julia heard Peter telling Margaret in a calm, but authoritative voice, to put the knife down on the floor, but before he had even finished the sentence, the door at the other end of the lounge opened and a handsome, middle aged man with wet hair, wearing a bathrobe came into the room. Peter's immediate thought was how much like Robert he looked. As Erik stared at the extraordinary scene unfolding in front of him, Margaret screamed, dropped the knife and fell to her knees sobbing wildly. Mathew, who had been standing next to Peter, reacted quickly and took the handkerchief out of his jacket's top pocket and quickly went across to where Margaret was now crying uncontrollably and picked up the knife, wrapping it in the handkerchief.

"Thank you Matt," Peter said, "please call the police now."

By now, Erik was holding Julia and comforting her in his arms. Peter went over to Margaret and helped her up off the floor and sat her down on the sofa.

"I think it might be best if Julia went into the kitchen." Peter's request was directed at Erik, who nodded and left the room with her.

Peter found himself alone with Margaret in the lounge, whilst Mathew was on his mobile phone in the hallway giving the police operator as much information as he could. Margaret had calmed down by now and was looking at Peter quizzically as he sat down in the armchair opposite her.

"I knew you had discovered the truth when I saw you looking at the photograph of Tara that night, it was the look of surprise on your face. Robert told me earlier today that you knew her in Oxford," Margaret said quietly, "how did you know I was here?"

"Robert rang me and told me he thought you were going to harm Julia." Peter replied and the look on Margaret's face when he told her, reminded him that it was time that

182

he rang Robert to let him know that Julia was safe and to find out if he was alright. Mathew had come back into the lounge by this time and told Peter that the police would be arriving in the next few minutes. After checking that Julia and Erik were alright in the kitchen, Peter left Margaret with Mathew and headed to the hallway, where he dialed Robert's mobile number. It was answered immediately.

"Peter, is that you, what's happened?" Peter could hear the anxiety in Robert's voice.

"Julia is safe Bob, just a bit shaken, in fact, everyone is safe but we are waiting for the police to arrive." Peter could almost hear the relief on the other end of the line, "I'm afraid it's very likely that Margaret will be arrested, it seems that I arrived with Matt at the apartment just in time, she was in the lounge threatening Julia with a knife."

"Christ, what a day." Robert sighed.

"What about you, where are you?" Peter asked.

"I'm in hospital in Ancona, shotgun wound in my leg and a sore head, I hit something when I fell, I'll be alright," Robert paused, "Peter, thank you for what you've done today, whatever Margaret and I have done Julia didn't deserve any of this."

"No, she didn't." Peter replied.

183

CHAPTER TWENTY-FOUR

TWO MONTHS LATER

It was towards the end of September and the weather had been unusually warm and humid for the time of year in London. Peter and Mathew were enjoying lunch in *The Elephant and Castle*. Since Peter had provided the police with a full statement of everything he knew concerning the Coleville affair, as it had become known in the newspapers, he had heard very little about the case. That was until yesterday when, unexpectedly, Patricia Coleville visited him at his home in Marylebone.

"That must have been a surprise old boy!" Mathew commented.

"Yes, it was a bit, she told me she had been upset and had been blaming herself for what had happened, all because she had found those photographs of Julia and Erik in the attic."

"She's being a bit hard on herself, there's only two people to blame for this whole mess I would say and neither of them is Patricia!" Mathew suggested.

"Exactly, but feelings of guilt can be difficult to deal with you know, Patricia used her mobile phone to take copies of the photos you see Matt and carelessly let Margaret discover them whilst they were away together in Italy. When Margaret saw them, she brushed it off, by telling Patricia they were just pictures of a young woman that Robert had a brief affair with many years ago and that she knew all about it". Peter explained.

"So, that was the moment when Margaret realised that she had been betrayed by Robert. Poor Patricia, she must have been horrified when she discovered the real truth behind the photographs." Mathew commented.

"She was, but I hope I put her mind at rest Matt. I told her that I had discovered her in-laws' secret long before she found the photos. In fact, what finding them did, was to put the wind up Robert Coleville and lead to Margaret finding out that she had been betrayed and that her real son was alive." Peter explained.

"I suppose you could say that Margaret seeing the photos did us a favour, it brought the whole matter to a head. I still can't believe the Coleville's would have gone to the police voluntarily and told them the truth though, do you?" Mathew asked.

"I'm not sure, Robert told me he was going to talk to Margaret about it and I'm not sure why, but I believed him. He didn't really have much choice, after all, I'd told him that if they didn't go to the police, then I would." Peter said. "Interestingly, Patricia told me that Simon has taken the whole episode quite well and although he doesn't want to see Margaret at present, he was relaxed about seeing Robert. He's actually visited Simon and Patricia in Hampstead a number of times over the past few months."

"What on earth did Robert say to them?" Mathew asked.

"He told them what he had told me when I last saw him in Oxford, the truth and Simon and Patricia both feel quite sympathetic towards him. Simon's view is that he has been a good father to him. As Sidney Newman used to tell us Matt, people can do some very bad things in their life, but it doesn't necessarily mean they're entirely wicked."

"He was certainly stupid not going to the police when Margaret came home with another mother's baby, that's for sure!" Mathew said.

"What really surprised me though, is that Simon, Patricia and Emily have been to see Julia and Erik!" Peter said.

"So Simon has finally met his real mother then."
Mathew smiled.

"Indeed, and apparently, the reunion went very well. As far as Julia and Erik are concerned nothing has changed between them, they are still mother and son and always will be, but they were both warm and affectionate towards Simon and his family. After all, Simon and Patricia are as much the victims in this dreadful story as Julia and Erik are. Another happy outcome is that Julia met her granddaughter!"

"Oh of course, I hadn't thought of that! And did Julia mention to Patricia the part you have played uncovering the story?" Mathew asked with a wry smile.

"Sort of, Julia told them that she thought that I played the part of an investigative journalist who needs a new accountant extremely well!" Peter laughed.

Robert parked his car on Old Lydd Road near to Camber Sands. He had driven from the country cottage in Sussex, where he had been living since returning from Italy. He had spent a few days in Chelsea on his immediate return, but found that the media had started bothering him since Margaret's arrest and he had decided he would be less conspicuous living in the cottage, away from London. Margaret had been released on bail, pending further enquiries and was staying with a cousin in Hampshire. Robert had been interviewed by the police in connection with Simon's abduction in 1973 and he was waiting to hear whether he would face any charges. Margaret was facing a number of charges. As well as the ongoing police investigation concerning the abduction, she was likely to be charged with threatening with an offensive weapon, following the drama at Julia's home in Bayswater. The Italian authorities also wanted to interview her regarding the theft of a shotgun and a reported shooting in Le Marche. On his return from the market, Maurizio had found Robert

186

on the kitchen floor of the farmhouse and had taken him to hospital. Following Robert's discharge, the hospital authorities had become suspicious and contacted the Carabinieri, who had opened an investigation. Maurizio had been interviewed and told them that his shotgun had been taken from his property without his permission, fired and then returned.

After buying his parking ticket and sticking it on the inside of the windscreen, Robert made his way down to the seafront. His limp was quite pronounced, due to the shooting and he felt self-conscious about it when people stared at him. This was all forgotten though, when he spotted the lone figure on the shore turn around and wave to him.

"I didn't think you would come." Robert said when he reached the shore. Julia was smiling as he approached her.

"Well I'm here!" Julia seemed calm and self-assured, Robert thought to himself, these were some of the reasons that he loved her so much.

"I don't deserve it," Robert had tears in his eyes, "my behaviour towards you when we first met was disgraceful, I deceived you Julia."

"Yes, you did and at first, when I read your letter, I was very angry with you." Julia spoke quietly. "But you deceived me all those years ago because you wanted to keep in touch with your son, I may have done the same myself, under the circumstances."

"I know, I'm so sorry Julia," Robert stammered, "Within a few weeks of us meeting I had fallen in love with you though and I've loved you ever since."

"You see Robert," and Julia smiled, "in a way, I deceived you as well when we were first met. I was penniless, in a foreign country, with a newborn baby to care for and you were wealthy and were prepared to take great risks to help me. I understand now why you took those risks. I didn't love you for some while, but I was happy to befriend you because you could help me and more importantly, help Erik. It took me a few years before I fell in love with you."

Robert took Julia's hand.

"I heard that you were shot and that your first thought when you recovered consciousness was for my safety," Julia continued, "does your leg still hurt, you have a limp?"

"It's nothing. Waiting to hear that you were safe was the worst time of my life, the wait seemed to go on forever. When Peter called me I was so relieved, even though I didn't ever think I would see you again." Robert told her.

"That Peter Wilson's a cool customer!" Julia laughed and Robert smiled.

"I understand Simon, Pat and Emily have been to see you." Robert said.

"They're a lovely family Robert, you're very lucky to have them. Simon is my son and we will always have a special bond and he's your son as well, you brought him up and did a good job by the look of things. I'm looking forward to getting to know him better, we have a lot of time to catch up on! I guess I now have two sons and a beautiful granddaughter!" Julia took Robert's arm and they walked together along the shore.

"And Erik, have you spoken with him?" Robert asked nervously.

"He knows everything Robert, he said he remembers you when he was little and liked you, he said you were always kind to us. Anyway, he said he wants to meet his father again." Julia smiled.

Taraneh Saderzadeh had been for a meeting in Notting Hill with the freeholder of her father's Kensington apartment. The meeting had gone well and she would speak with her father about extending the lease when she returned to Tehran. It was a warm September afternoon and she had decided to enjoy the sunshine and meander through the backstreets of Kensington, rather than taking a cab, on her way back home to the apartment. She should have known better, she thought to herself, because when she had reached Gordon Place the heavens opened. She cursed herself for not carrying an umbrella, she was in London for goodness sake! By the time she had reached the corner of Holland Street, the rain was torrential and there was nothing for it but to take shelter in the little pub on the corner. She had passed it many times over the years and whilst she had always thought it looked very pleasant, she had never ventured inside. Now was her chance she thought and she rushed through the little garden up to the front door, which was wide open. In her haste to get out of the rain, she almost collided with one of the customers, who was carefully carrying a pint of beer in each hand and heading back to his table. Luckily, he had spotted her rushing through the door and managed to sidestep her, whilst still holding on to the beers, although some did splash on the floor.

"I am so sorry!" Taraneh blurted out, feeling a bit stupid, but also noticing the man holding the beers was quite handsome, tall, slim and dressed quite fashionably.

"Not at all, you look drenched." the handsome man said sympathetically.

Taraneh just stared at him, it was his accent, strong Birmingham, Brummie that was what they called it she remembered. She hadn't heard it spoken since she was a nurse years and years ago. For what seemed like an age, but was probably only a matter of seconds, they both stared at each other.

"Peter, you're Peter from Oxford!" Taraneh said slipping off her wet coat. Peter's face lit up.

"What an incredible coincidence, we've just been talking about you, you're Taraneh Saderzadeh! How wonderful to see you again, please come and join us we're sat over there." Peter nodded to the table where Mathew was sat waiting for his drink. Taraneh stared open-mouthed at Peter, wondering to herself why on earth they had been talking about her.

"I'm sorry Taraneh, perhaps you are meeting someone here?" Peter asked as they made their way over to the table.

"No, no, I'm just surprised to see you and intrigued to know why, after more than forty years, you have been talking about me!" Taraneh laughed.

"Come and meet Mathew and everything will become clear, I promise!" Peter said and handed Mathew his drink.

"Mathew, may I introduce Taraneh Saderzadeh, Taraneh…Mathew." Peter announced. Mathew stood up to greet her.

"Delighted to meet you Taraneh, I've heard a lot about you!" he smiled and after asking what she would like to drink, disappeared towards the bar.

"Well come on, tell me!" Taraneh said impatiently.

"Do you remember that story you told me about the time you were working as a nanny in Hampstead?"

"My word, what a memory you have Peter Wilson!" Taraneh said.

"And yours isn't too bad either, remembering my surname after all this time!" Peter laughed and noticed that Taraneh was blushing slightly.

Peter took out his mobile phone and showed Taraneh the photograph of her with the Coleville's, holding baby Simon.

"That's incredible! Where on earth did you get that from?" Taraneh asked still staring at the photograph. By this time, Mathew had returned and handed her a large gin and tonic.

"It's a long story Taraneh, perhaps I can tell it to you over dinner one evening?" Peter asked.

"I've only been here five minutes and you're asking me out to dinner!" Taraneh smiled. "That would be delightful Peter!"

"So, cheers everyone, old friends!" Mathew said, raising his pint glass.

Printed in Great Britain
by Amazon

61513344R00112